RELEASING SHADOWS

SHIRLEY HEDRICK WILLIAMS

FIRE and GRACE
Publishing, LLC

Shirley Hedrick Williams
FIRE and GRACE Publishing, LLC
fireandgracepublishing.com

First Edition 2021
First Printing 2021

ISBN: 978-1-7349381-8-0

Edited by Michelle Areaux and Melissa Plantz
Cover Design by VC Book Cover Design

Other Books by Shirley Hedrick Williams from FIRE and GRACE Publishing, LLC

Awakening Crow Moon: and Other Poems and Short Stories

In memory of my Dad, Shirley Lee Hedrick, Jr., who shared the life of Christ with me through the wonders of nature, and by the way he lived his life.

And

In memory of my Mother, Ada Mae Buckley Hedrick, who taught me to use the measure of faith God bestows. She blessed my soul by singing hymns while she went about her daily housework or while sitting at her sewing machine.

Both took the time to answer my many questions about God, His Son Jesus, the Holy Spirit and Heaven. I am forever grateful to God for such loving parents; and love them greatly in return.

CHAPTER ONE

Sleet pelted the windshield; and the wipers scratched the surface as they slid across their limited space. The headlights glowed eerily. Trying to concentrate through the onslaught of a severe winter, Kailynn squinted. The road rose up a narrow strip like a dark rope winding around the snow packed West Virginia mountains. Suddenly, the hood of a white car appeared ghostlike out of nowhere. Fright streaked from her heart into her mind. Knowing even as she did it that her reflex was wrong, she pressed her foot firmly on the brake. At once, she began skidding sideways. The white automobile swerved also as if to miss her, slid and flipped over the embankment. Screeching metal and exploding glass screamed that a car had struck the railroad tracks below.

Another vehicle managed to stop just as Kailynn gained control of her car. Now it loomed colorless in the night. A sickening quietness echoed the swishing noise of wind and sleet. Numb with shock, she groped in her handbag for her cell phone. It wasn't there. She pictured it plugged into the charger on her bedside table.

Unbuckling the seat belt, she emerged from the small red car with dread. Her jacket shielded her back somewhat and the toboggan her head, but her sweat pants and walking shoes were no match for the wet, icy weather. She climbed down part of the way, and then found herself sliding down the embankment toward the overturned car. Crawling around until she could peer into a window, Kailynn's heart jumped as a woman's head turned toward her. The dark eyes tried to focus before closing in unconsciousness.

"Are they pinned in there?" The driver who had stopped on the road strained to look into the window. "Yeah, they sure are!" Answering his own question, he removed his coal company cap and wiped his forehead with his denim sleeve. "There's a man pinned on the driver's side behind an airbag, but I don't see any other passengers." Grabbing a handle, he grunted with the attempt to force a door open. Finally standing up, he ran the back of a hand over his mouth, a man yearning to physically leap to their aid but incapable in this circumstance. "I called for help on the cell phone. They should be here soon…" His words trailed off in the wind.

They stood looking up at the road, both wondering how long it would really take help to arrive.

Later, Kailynn sat in her car, shaking more from nerves than the cold temperature, while an emergency crew cut the injured couple out of the mangled metal. The man who had called for help leaned against his blue Chevy Blazer, talking to the police; and her little red Toyota was just another car in the short line forming on the ridge. When the ambulance pulled off squealing its siren even though it, too, had to slow down for the curves, she followed at a distance.

The emergency room was crowded and noisy. Restless children whined, waiting with one parent while doctors checked their mother or father or a sibling. A baby girl with blond curls tousled on her pretty head surprisingly slept soundly on her father's broad shoulder. Elderly people waited stoically for their turn, some obviously having endured pain many times in their senior years.

Kailynn could imagine the rush when the ambulance arrived with the accident victims. She envisioned the immediate attention of doctors and nurses, the medical instruments, the tests if time allowed. How would she know if the staff moved the couple to intensive care? How would she know if they died? *Oh God,* she breathed a prayer.

After an hour of sitting, too warm in her gray sweatshirt, jacket and toboggan, she made her way to the front desk. A harried young woman looked up from the papers she was filling out. She arched her eyebrows under her disheveled bangs instead of asking a question.

"I…I…,"…" Kailynn began. "I'm wondering about the couple who came in the ambulance tonight…the couple in the car wreck."

The woman's light eyes widened, but her tone of voice remained calm. "The Websters? Intensive Care. Second floor. You'll have to use the phone up in the waiting room to talk to the nurses." When Kailynn turned on her heel instantly, not even saying thank you, she looked relieved. One less.

Before entering the elevator to the second floor, Kailynn made a quick dash into the women's room. After running the water until it was warm, she wiped her face with a paper towel. Her eyes stared starkly back at her in the mirror more green than blue, the shade they always turned when emotions, especially anxiety, took over her features. She held the damp paper towel over her face for a few minutes.

On walking through the door of the waiting room upstairs, she smelled freshly brewed coffee. A tall lady with red hair poured the black liquid into a styrofoam cup. As she barely sipped, she looked toward the two obviously distraught children at the other end of the room. Kailynn followed her gaze to the sobbing little girl leaning against the boy's tensed arm. The petite blonde girl, still in pajamas and a pink jacket, looked to be about seven. The boy, dressed in a white tee-shirt, blue jeans and a gray hoodie appeared to be in his very early teens.

When Kailynn started for the telephone on the wall, the woman stepped in front of her and grasped the receiver. Placing her cup on a nearby table, she tapped a button with a long index fingernail. "Yes. This is the Webster's neighbor. The children are eager to learn of their condition." She glanced again in their direction. "Oh, should I take them home with me then? My name is Agnes Naylor. Let me give you my number; and please call if there is any change one way or another. Mrs. Webster's sister may not be able to be here until later."

As the woman rattled her telephone number off, Kailynn's eyes took in the children's confused expressions. *"Lord,"* she thought, *why did I have to be a part of all this pain and confusion? Why didn't I stay home tonight? Why did I think I could outrun my own problems only to bring horrific pain to others?* Confusion creased her dark brows, too, as she yanked off the toboggan and lowered her head. How had she played a part in this nightmare? What happened? Did her car slide first or was the road so slippery in that one area at that hour of the night that both cars lost control? Even as the woman left the room with the children, she agonized over these questions.

Sitting there alone she found it necessary to reason that the icy road could just as easily have wrecked her car. She could have been the victim. Why should she blame herself in any way for this tragic occurrence? The authorities didn't think her car had caused the accident. Why should she? She rose to look out the window. Snow covered all the vehicles parked below. *I am concerned. That is all there is to it. It's only natural I would be concerned.* She reasoned further and muttered under her breath. Finally, she went to the telephone and clicked the number indicated on a sign on the wall.

"Intensive Care Unit," a professional, but pleasing female voice answered.

"I'm calling about the Websters."

"Oh, you made it sooner than expected. Push the red button outside the double doors. Mr. and Mrs. Webster are in the first two rooms respectively. I'm sorry, but you can only have fifteen minutes with each."

Puzzled, she still couldn't resist seeing them for herself. With a racing heart, she hurried across the hall; and with a trembling hand, hit the large red button. As soon as she had pushed it, the two doors swung open. She moved quickly inside, yet as soon as she entered she slowed, searching for the desk and relieved to see it in the middle of the hall and not too close to the first room. Entering the room, she saw a camera pointing toward the bed, a television and a nurse checking tubes.

The nurse nodded at her and left the room.

Barely inside the room, Kailynn froze. Holding her breath, she forced herself to look at the figure in the bed. She felt her heart thud as she recognized the face on the pillow. The closed eyes looked peaceful but the respirator distorted the mouth, and the rise and fall of the lungs was grotesque. The brown hair was damp at the temples. Kailynn longed to stroke her temples and somehow try to comfort her. Perhaps, the woman would sense that she was sorry and yearned for a chance to change the circumstances. Her desire to act upon this thought was interrupted by the nurse's presence.

Kailynn turned her back to avoid questions. She decided to duck into the next room where Mr. Webster should lie, but as she did attendants were rolling his bed out and talking about surgery. His handsome head with its blond hair streaked with silver lay motionless at the top of a white blanket pulled up to his chin, yet his deep blue eyes were open, blinking slowly. Her body felt numb as she followed the bed to the elevator, then made her legs move her away to the waiting room doors and away from the hospital.

As she pulled out of the parking lot, her hands were trembling and her knees felt weak. She didn't want to drive this little car now, but she wouldn't want to alarm her parents further by calling them to come after her. Snow began to fall again when she drove through South Charleston, Spring Hill and along Kanawha River. She kept recalling the reason she had taken off driving in the first place. It was actually the day she should enter the Medical Center for tests and finally, the preparation for her heart operation, a long awaited procedure. In anxiety she had felt like running far away, knowing full well she would eventually return on time for her parents' peace of mind. They had waited for this day for years. Now she was late and they were probably out of their minds with worry though, as usual, they wouldn't let it show.

Her mother, clad in a blue winter coat, ran out of the old white house, her salt and pepper hair wet with snow when Kailynn managed to park to one side in the wide driveway of their St. Albans home. No doubt her mother had gone to her room to check on her daughter as she had for a number of years since the doctors had informed her that her daughter's heart had a defective valve. She had often asked, "Why do you take these chances?"

The answer was always the same, "I think while I'm driving." Indeed, she did think about her life as she walked or drove among the hills viewing the skies in daytime or the moon at night. Most often she felt peace too, but not this time. This time she had driven into a snow storm. This time she should have stayed home to think or kneel beside her bed to pray.

"Oh Honey, I've been looking for you!" An expression of mingled relief and hope glistened in Mae's light blue eyes.

Kailynn stepped out of the car. "Sorry, Mom. I forgot my cell phone or I would have called.

"You were expected at the Medical Center today, Kailynn."

Yes, she remembered her reason for driving blindly through the snow, but she stared in disbelief into her mother's anxious face. *Not tonight*, she silently pleaded to herself. *Not tonight…not so suddenly. I need time to think about this.*

"I have your bag packed. Your dad will pull the car out. We need to go, Hon." She took hold of her daughter's bluish cheeks the way she had always done from the day Kailynn could remember. "Trust in God, Kailynn. He works in many ways."

Her white-haired father strode briskly toward the garage. She stared silently at the back of his brown leather jacket and inhaled a deep breath. She felt tired...tired of being tired. *Dear God,* she prayed. *I'm sorry. Forgive my mistakes. This night is so strange, but please take charge and be Lord of my life. You never make mistakes. You are sovereign and I can trust in Jesus' name.*

Lee backed the Ford Taurus cautiously out of the garage; and leaning over the seat, opened the passenger door for her. He nodded gravely, beseeching with dark eyes. Having settled her daughter in the front, Mae sat in the back so that he could talk with his daughter. Instead, Kailynn haltingly related her narrow escape on the road, apologizing for the worry she caused them. As always, they accepted her apology with unconditional love.

At the hospital, that look of hope in her mother's eyes strengthened her resolve to endure the blood tests and chest x-rays as well as more uncomfortable situations. On the morning of her surgery, she actually felt somewhat refreshed as she showered with a special cleansing soap. By the time surgeons explained to her about the heart lung machine and functions of all the tubes she would need after the operation, she felt so physically and mentally weary that the explanations didn't really prepare her for the reality. She only knew that if this operation were successful, blood-flow through her heart and lungs would increase circulation and oxygen. The wait was over, not because her body was stronger but because her health would dangerously decline without surgery.

Kailynn finally forced her eyes to open a little and thought she saw a lovely woman in a yellow dress at the foot of the bed. She closed her eyes. When she opened them again, she saw the large yellow balloon tied to the foot of her bed and her mother standing there in a white hospital gown and mask saying something comforting that Kailynn couldn't understand. She slipped back into the safe, silent world behind her closed eyelids. She must rest. She still had a long road of medication and examinations to undergo, but she had a chance to live past forty years. She would live. She could now really live. Suddenly, she felt probing fingers and cold instruments; and heard voices talking about low blood pressure.

CHAPTER TWO

Gone, the blue tinge she was accustomed to view in the mirror. Roses bloomed in her cheeks as well as her neighborhood as she enjoyed summer walks on the steep streets of St. Albans, yet always her joy led to prayers for the Webster family. When Fall rolled around, she boarded a bus to Charleston. She couldn't bring herself to drive her car, though she appreciated her dad keeping up the maintenance as well as the insurance. She remembered the excitement in picking out the red Toyota, the color reflecting the spunky spirit suppressed by her frail body. When she stepped off the bus onto the busy city street, she followed her heart to a Christian book store she had seen advertised in the local newspaper. Roderick Webster was listed as owner. She wore a blue fedora to cover her hair and pulled her lightweight, cream-colored jacket closer as if for security while she stood there chilling nearly half an hour in front of the plate glass window. She gazed longingly at beautifully framed pictures illustrating the birth, life, death and resurrection of Jesus Christ and lovely book displays.

A salesgirl with short blond hair and wearing a large red sweater opened the door.

"May we help you?"

"I…I'm looking for a job." Kailynn said.

The girl's face lit up with a smile. "Well, please come inside!"

As she entered, Kailynn saw Roderick Webster standing at the end of the high counter. His posture was straight in a charcoal bulky sweater. His blond hair was streaked with more silver strands. He looked through the same morning edition of the newspaper she had read.

"Hey, Rod, we have someone looking for a job!"

The salesgirl sounded a bit too eager; and Kailynn couldn't hide her surprise as she shifted her gaze from the man's face to the girl's excited expression.

"Oh, sorry. My name is Carla Turner. I'm happy to see you because tomorrow is my last day; and we haven't had anyone to apply for the job."

At this, Rod's blue eyes darkened a little in Carla's direction as his mouth tightened in a grin.

"I've been with the store for ten years," Carla explained, "but my baby is just about due. My husband and I decided it would be better if I stayed with the baby after she is born. Ever since we placed the ad I've been praying for someone to take my place."

"I'm glad to meet you, Carla. I'm Kailynn Richardson, and I've been praying for a job!" She smiled broadly.

"Woo Hoo!" Carla's voice sounded insistent. "Rod, she may be the answer to our prayers!"

He looked at Kailynn for the first time. "Have you had any experience in retail?"

She was somewhat shocked at first by his slight speech impediment, but she could understand his words perfectly.

"No sir. I like books and people, and I like to type."

He looked at her thoughtfully. "Well, no bad habits to break. How do you feel about an interview right now?"

"That's fine," she answered, taking the application Carla handed to her.

As she sat beside his desk in a back office watching his eyes scan the completed application, she noticed the small hearing aid in his right ear. There was, she realized, a deliberate attempt to cover it with hair he had let grow a little since she had seen him that fateful night. She slipped the hat from her head revealing the dark auburn hair cut in layers around her face. His eyes lifted from the sheet and stared intently for a few seconds. She automatically wondered if he recognized her.

"You look awfully young," he observed.

"I'm older than I look." She sat up straighter in her chair.

"So I see," he said, looking back down at the paper. "Well, that doesn't really matter." He waved his hand holding a pen. "I was just thinking out loud, I guess."

Kailynn nodded. She knew she was bone thin, though she was starting to gain a bit more weight.

"Why were you homeschooled in your junior year?"

"Ill…illness," she stammered.

"You attended State?"

"Yes, sir. A few courses at a time." Was he thinking she couldn't talk to customers? "And I took some courses online from Marshall," she added.

"Why do you want to work in a Christian book store?"

Her lips parted in a shy smile. "Bible literature fascinates me, thanks to my Dad, and I think the paintings and music are inspirational. I'd like a chance to share with people."

He straightened his shoulders and appeared pleased. "You know we consider this store a ministry, but it is still a business. There's a lot of work involved in keeping it going at a sufficient financial rate. We compete with shopping malls and discount chains which is where the young people seem to be standing in line for jobs."

Again she nodded. Why couldn't she be herself? She realized the threat to small businesses no matter the quality of service. If he only knew how strongly she felt and how much she wanted to help his store succeed. The burden the accident must have caused! Yet he would probably be appalled to learn the reason for her earnest desire.

Her blue-green eyes met his and then lowered as if he might read her thoughts.

He continued,, "The truth is there are special benefits in both types of stores depending on what the customer wants and needs. Part of your job would be to convince him through your service that special attention is more important than bargains, that knowledge which I pass on to you is more valuable than speedy checkout."

He hesitated as he consulted a calendar on the wall to one side of the desk. "Could you start training tomorrow?"

She took a quick breath before answering. "Yes, sir."

"The first lesson you must learn is to make friendly eye contact with your customer." Their eyes met and held, and she smiled shyly.

~ ~ ~

The next day she followed Carla around the store. Wearing one of the blue smocks, she dusted and stocked the shelves with new books. In the afternoon she learned to use the cash register.

"When Emma Webster worked here everything ran smoothly and we did pretty well," Carla told her. "But after the car accident that took her life, Rod needed time to recuperate and adjust." She shrugged her shoulders. "I suppose my best just wasn't good enough. We failed to catch up with technology or purchase modern equipment and lost business as a result."

Kailynn realized she was staring at Carla's face so she made herself blink as calmly as possible. "It...it... must have been difficult for you...to suddenly find yourself in charge." She watched Carla nod peering at her strangely; and then hoping to cover the fact that she had just received alarming news, she deliberately took hold of her emotions. "I mean, you had to do their work when necessary as well as your own. Don't blame yourself for something you couldn't help. I'm sure you did your best, and the store is still here and open."

Relaxing, Carla smiled at that last fact.

The two women took their lunch break at a conference table in the back of the store, eating grilled chicken sandwich meals Carla had picked up for them. Their boss sat on a stool at the front counter going over invoices. He was quiet all morning, greeting them softly when they arrived and speaking in low tones to Carla. For the most part, he trusted her to train their new employee.

"Kailynn," Carla spoke between bites. "Today is my last day officially working, but I'm going to stop in every day for a while to see if you need help with anything. Rod plans to hire another full time person and a part time employee as soon as business gets better. Until then, just take it one day at a time."

"Thank you," Kailynn said sincerely. "I'll look forward to seeing you."

The first morning without Carla, the proprietor Roderick Webster greeted Kailynn cordially and offered her a seat beside his desk, bowing his head to ask God's blessing on the day.

She actually began to enjoy keeping busy, including the tiny details of pricing and boxing up merchandise for delivery or unpacking new merchandise. Propping up copies of new books to display throughout the store, she spotted Rod answering the telephone at the front counter. Still holding a hard-cover book in both hands, she stopped as she became aware of his silence and noticed the color draining from his handsome face. She saw him replace the phone on the charger, his blue eyes darting around the room in perplexity. Did she dare ask him who called and what they said to him? Deciding it would be an unwise thing to do, her mind, in spite of her abhorrence, traveled back to that tragic night.

From the moment of that mysterious phone call her boss took while she was setting up displays everything seemed to go wrong for a while. First the register broke down. Rod managed to pull the drawer, but checkouts would have to be done by hand until the machine could be serviced. Her first customer when she began using a receipt pad happened to be none other than Agnes Naylor, Rod's neighbor, whose black rain coat contrasted attractively with her red hair. When she first walked up to the counter with a couple of small booklets, Kailynn recognized her immediately. Holding the pen sideways she raised it nervously to her chin. The pale blue eyes looked past her toward the office.

Kailynn, not daring to raise her own eyes again, quickly placed the bill she offered in the rightful slot in the drawer, wrote down the sum of the two booklets plus tax and proceeded to give her change for a ten.

"What are you doing?!" Agnes asked.

"I beg your pardon?"

"I gave you a twenty dollar bill and you tried to short me!"

Kailynn looked down at the drawer, saw tens and twenties and honestly didn't know which bill the lady had given her.

"What's the problem?" Rod hurried out of his office.

"Oh Rod! This woman tried to steal from me. I gave her a twenty for these booklets and she only gave me change for a ten!"

He turned to Kailynn, waiting for an explanation.

"I thought she handed me a ten, Mr. Webster."

At that, Agnes leaned threateningly across the counter, her face red. "I could slap you for that!"

"Agnes." Rod controlled her rising anger with a whisper. "Kailynn is new and this is her first day working here. Let's give her a break."

"Sorry, Rod." Agnes' tone of voice radically softened. "I thought she was trying to short me. I didn't mean to cause *you* a problem" She showed her beautiful white teeth, but her eyes, fringed in long black lashes, failed to express a change in mood as she continued browsing through the store.

"Agnes Naylor! It's good to see you!" A woman with brown hair cut stylishly around her face exclaimed as she entered the store.

"Well, Nadine! When did you arrive in town?"

"About an hour ago. I stopped at Rod's house, and when he wasn't home I thought he might be working at the shop."

Rod rounded the counter and gave the woman a light kiss on the cheek. Turning to Kailynn, he smiled. "Kailynn Richardson, this is my sister-in-law, Nadine Thomas, my wife's older sister."

"Oh, don't make me sound so old, Rod!" Nadine laughed.

Grinning, he asked, "Are you going to stay at our house for a few days this time?"

Loosening the buttons of her navy-blue coat, she shook her head. "Nope. I checked into the hotel. You know I like to stay close to the shops, but I'm anxious to see my sister's children."

"Dinner at our house this evening then?"

Kailynn noticed a resemblance to Emma in her hazel eyes as she nodded agreement. "I'll look around here, and do some shopping in the mall, and meet you at the house."

"That's great. The kids will be happy to see you."

The rest of the day was uneventful except for an elderly man who wanted to purchase a Bible. Kailynn observed his hands tremble as he bent his white head over the shelves, leafing through large type pages. She reached upon a higher shelf for a leather Bible, a bit larger than the other books, but the print was large and clear. As she placed the book in his hands his face brightened, and then looked apologetically at her.

"This is nice, ma'am, but I better look at some of the cheaper Bibles."

She ran her fingers over the cover before re-opening the book. "This Bible will last someone a long time. The words of Christ are not only in red, but clear and readable."

The man's face already shone with pleasure as he read, "What would a man give for his soul."

Her voice lowered. "This is a book that will endure and witness to others in time to come." She knew the joy he would experience handling this book every day, how precious it would be to him and how much he would desire to leave it to someone he loved, someone who needed it when he would pass from this earthly life. Respectfully, though, she replaced the Bible.

The man returned to the first shelf, but as she started to walk away he called her back. "I think I'll take that Bible after all."

While checking him out, she realized that Roderick had been observing the entire conversation with interest from his usual spot at the end of the counter. She placed the bills the man handed her beside the drawer until she had counted his change. Her boss' eyebrows lifted; and he and Kailynn grinned at each other.

At closing time, she observed Rod locking up the store, and walking back to his office to take care of paperwork. She was taking off her smock to hang it up in the back hall when she saw him standing at his desk looking at a piece of paper.

All the color faded from his face again as he wadded it up and threw it in the trash can beside his desk. He rushed toward the exit. "Lock the back door behind you, Kailynn."

When he had left, curiosity led her into the office. She picked up the paper and unfolded it. In penmanship displaying widely looped letters the words formed a short invitation, *Join me.*

A movement over her shoulder made her jump as Carla said, "That's Emma's handwriting.

CHAPTER THREE

It wasn't until the following day that she finally had occasion to see the children. They came into the store with their jackets open, carrying textbooks although their backpacks appeared full.

"Hey! Are you Kailynn?" The boy was direct.

"Yes, I am."

His brow lowered and his hazel eyes didn't leave her face. A memory replayed itself across his youthful features. "You were at the hospital when my mother died. You were in the waiting room."

The little girl who had stopped inside the door moved closer to the counter, her blond hair spilling around her curious brown eyes. "Did you lose someone too that night?" She piped up.

Kailynn could hardly find her voice. "No…" She shook her head slowly. Sadness shadowed her vision.

The little girl's eyes widened meaningfully. "You're really lucky. It's awful hard to lose your mom. I'm Milly. My brother's name is Taylor. Do your friends call you Kailie?" Before she could answer, Rod came out of the office; and he and the two children left for home.

The days began to pass swiftly as Kailynn, for the first time in her life, kept busy with a variety of tasks. The store closed early on Wednesdays because there were prayer meetings and Bible studies at most of the churches in the area. It was closed all day on Sundays and she spent that whole day with her mother and father at their church service and dinner at home. She couldn't help wondering about the Webster family's day of worship.

On Monday, when straightening a few paintings unique for their haunting blue and turquoise Postimpressionist style with twilight spreading over mountains and reflected on rivers, she noticed the artist's signature. *R Webster.*

"That's one of Rod's," Carla's voice whispered over Kailynn's left shoulder. "He's really a talented artist, mostly illustrating scenic views instead of doing the portraits he enjoyed when Emma was alive. He expresses himself more in paint since he lost his singing voice in the accident."

Kailynn turned her head, her eyes staring at Carla with a stricken expression.

"Are you okay, Kailynn? What's wrong?"

Kailynn's throat constricted when she tried to answer. Tears welled up in her eyes.

"Let me help you to the restroom."

Once inside the restroom, Kailynn leaned against the sink and sobbed. *Oh God, they lost so much! Please, please help me to make a difference. I can't change what happened. I'm not sure it was my fault, but if I hadn't been there maybe…maybe…it wouldn't have happened. All I know at this point is I must help them anyway I can. Just help me to do this, Lord! Please!*

Having splashed cold water on her face, carefully drying with paper towels, she squared her shoulders and steadied her legs before opening the door.

Thanksgiving week was upon them. The store would close Wednesday and Thursday. On Tuesday Roderick reorganized shelves, stopping to gaze out the plate glass window at the darkening clouds. During lunch, he sat in deep thought in his office sipping the hot chocolate Kailynn had poured from her thermos into his favorite cup bearing the title *coffee hound*. She glimpsed him through the open door, once in passing, picking up his children's pictures.

"Kailynn," he called her name as he locked the front door.

"Yes sir."

He turned, blue eyes finally focusing attention on her face. "I have a favor to ask of you."

She nodded, waiting.

"Could you spend Thanksgiving Day with us?"

Oh no. Not that question! Not now. "I'm sorry, Mr. Webster, my parents have a special dinner planned this year with a few of my aunts and uncles." *I don't want to tell him they are thanking God for my surgery and recovery,* she thought.

"Would you like to join us?" She would endure his finding out if necessary.

"I want the children to have Thanksgiving at home. It's important."

"What about their grandparents?"

"My parents are deceased and Emma's parents enjoy the day in their old home place in Ohio. We always spent a couple of nights there before Christmas, but celebrated holidays in our own home."

She kept silent. She was letting him down! She couldn't believe this. She didn't have long to think because Agnes Naylor pecked happily on the window.

When Rod let her inside, she pulled her leather coat away from her throat and removed her gloves. "Rod, I hate to bother you here, but I need to know right away. Would you and the children have Thanksgiving with my brother and me? Perhaps in your home?"

Rod looked resigned to an uncertain destiny. "Thank you, Agnes. That sounds like an idea."

"Wonderful! I'll cook everything at my house and bring it over."

"No. Not the turkey. We would like to stuff and bake the turkey. I'll send some home with you."

"Oh, well, fine then. I'll cook vegetables and bake pies." Agnes was obviously elated, her beautiful smile brilliant. She left without acknowledging Kailynn who had stood practically between them.

"You'd better bundle up warmly, Kailynn." Roderick was gazing at the sky again. "It looks like wind clouds out there. Happy Thanksgiving."

~ ~ ~

One day, the week following Thanksgiving, Roderick introduced a man close to Kailynn's age during morning devotions. Robust good looks, dark curly hair and light eyes fringed with black eyelashes made for a handsome man. He had a cheerful demeanor in his blue and gold striped buttoned-down shirt, and reminded her of an Irish tenor she always enjoyed hearing at Gospel sings.

"Kailynn, this is Joey Jackson, Agnes Naylor's brother. Joey, Kailynn Richardson," Rod said.

She extended her hand in a friendly handshake when Rod quickly informed her, "He will be our new assistant manager. I'm not relinquishing the actual management of this business yet." The two men grinned at each other.

She felt her facial features freeze. "I'm glad to meet you, Mr. Jackson. I'd better straighten the shelves and dust before we open." She said no more all day, letting the men, for the most part, wait on people. She kept busy shelving, pricing, labeling and boxing items for the mail.

The devotions over the next morning, Roderick asked to speak to her in the office. "Kailynn, is something wrong?"

"What could be wrong?"

He was caught off guard. "Are you bothered because I hired Joey?"

"It's your shop, Mr. Webster. You may hire anyone you like."

"I'd like you to be honest with me, Kailynn. We've always had good rapport with our employees here."

Her eyes, more green than blue at this moment, glanced at the wall and then back to his puzzled face. "I understood you would hire another full time person, Mr. Webster, but an assistant manager? Shouldn't I have a chance at that position since you hired me first?"

Understanding raised his eyebrows and a half smile lifted the corners of his mouth. "I wasn't aware you were applying for a management position. Do you have any experience?"

"Has Mr. Jackson?"

Roderick looked annoyed at this response. "Yes, in departments, though the particulars are confidential unless he tells you."

"Well, how am I going to get experience if I don't have an opportunity?"

"Kailynn, experience comes in time. I hope you don't think I would overlook qualifications for any reason."

She pressed her lips together and shook her head. "I'm sorry, Mr. Webster. I'm not ashamed of my behavior, but I am bewildered. I didn't think any of this out." She rose, the composed woman he had come to know, but he had already seen the fire in her eyes.

In spite of herself, she enjoyed working with Joey. His warm, toothy smile and hearty laughter brightened the atmosphere along with the Christmas bells and bows they strung throughout the store. They adorned the plate glass window with large snowflakes and the door with a wreath welcoming the new customers who started milling around the store. She wrapped many gifts and boxed up parcels for delivery.

Just as she began to feel somewhat overwhelmed, nonetheless joyfully busy, Roderick and Joey hired a tiny dynamo named Sara Dawson. Long sandy hair pulled back at the sides with a barrette, light brown eyes and a wide smile topped a small boned frame that always seemed to be on the move. Her little bird-like fingers quickly labeled merchandise and ran the cash register. Her happy chatter with customers was as lively as her service. Sara was also quick to offer her services to Roderick's family when he presented a problem with his children.

"I have a prayer request this morning," Rod informed them all before their daily devotions. "I should go to a trade show this week. I've already paid to participate in a seminar. Since business is picking back up, I wanted to take advantage of this opportunity, but Agnes has the flu and can't keep the kids after all. Would you join me in prayer for someone to take care of them in my home while I'm gone? I'll personally pay a week's wages out of my own savings."

"Mr. Webster, I wouldn't mind if you could do without me here," Sara offered.

Kailynn's thoughts spun, thinking of her own opportunity to finally be of personal help to the Websters and the alternative, doing without Sara's rapid assistance at the store. She firmly intervened. "No, Sara, I don't think we can possibly do without your efficiency right now and still do as well. Let me stay with the children. I've wanted to spend time with them anyway."

Rod appeared immensely pleased.

Joey's extraordinary eyes showed surprise. "Well, Kailynn, you're valuable to me...to the store...too."

Rod cocked his head in Joey's direction, a lock of blond hair falling on his handsome forehead.

Wheels were turning in Joey's brain. "I've an idea. I could stop by some evenings to check on you and the children...to see if you need anything...and discuss any business or customers with you at that time. What do you say, Kailynn?"

She was relieved that she would be the one to stay with the children. "Sure, Joey. You're the assistant manager."

This affirmation elicited a healthy laugh from Joey. Rod, on the other hand, sat back, elbow on the arm of his chair, his index finger resting in the cleft of his chin, in thought.

CHAPTER FOUR

Emma sat on a patchwork quilt that covered dried October grass, an umbrella of red maple leaves sheltering her from the Indian summer sun. Her yellow dress swirled around the red and brown squares. Soft brown tendrils escaped her hair which was piled lightly upon her head. Only hints of white strands were visible in the sunlight. A peach blush enhanced her high cheekbones as her full lips parted in a smile. Golden flecks sparkled in her warm brown eyes as she raised her long fingers up to her rounded chin in amusement.

Her son stood before her in jeans and matching denim shirt over a blue tee-shirt. He leaned an arm on a branch. "Wanna mosey on home, Little Lady?"

She laughed happily at his effort at the manly impression.

His hazel eyes winked at her teasingly. Reaching down for an apple to sink his strong white teeth into, his sturdy jaw worked tirelessly as he chewed.

Suddenly, only the top of his dark head of hair appeared before the television screen went blue. When a picture formed again, her daughter stood in his place. Her honey blonde hair framed her baby face. She looked like she was posing in her long flowered dress until she realized the camera was scanning her bare feet. Embarrassed, she started motioning with her hands for her brother to raise the lens.

"Come here, Sweetheart, sit beside me." Her mother patted the quilt. The girl curled up close to her mother. They both looked into the camera, brown eyes shining with love, smiled and slowly waved.

The picture turned blue again, for the last time. Kailynn stared at the vacant screen, tears standing in her eyes. So, this was Emma's life, and in one night it was gone. It was a pity her husband wasn't there that Autumn day. She supposed the family had other videos, but this was the last. If they knew who Kailynn really was, she wouldn't be there long, she thought soberly. *Oh God, is this Your plan? Or is this my way of handling guilt? Please let me see clearly. And help me to be a blessing to this family.*

"Do you want to see our painting of Mommy?"

Kailynn jumped slightly at the sound of Milly's soft voice beside the armchair. The little girl, supposed to be sleeping in bed, stood in her white flannel nightgown, robe and fuzzy pink slippers, longing to show someone the mother she loved, longing to relive the warmth of her mother's love. Kailynn rose, pushing up the sleeves of her brown sweater as she took hold of the little hand Milly offered; and allowed herself to be led to the fireplace in the spacious room where a large portrait glowed with colors over the mantel. There were gold, yellow and crimson hues lighting that area of the lamp lit room.

Milly then led her to the enormous Christmas tree, and she recalled its evergreen scent greeting her at the front door this evening. The little girl pointed out ornaments she and her mother had made together. Some of these decorations held snapshots of each family member. The faces smiled up at them, carefree moments captured by camera.

"Mommy liked the star at the top of the tree. Every Christmas she would tell me the story of the wise men. See the angels circling the top of the tree? That's because angels announced the birth of baby Jesus to the shepherds and sang in the sky. The manger is down here under the tree because Jesus was God's most precious gift to us. That's what Mommy said."

"Your mommy is right. Jesus is God's most precious gift to us. Because He lived, died and rose again we can have eternal life."

They were both kneeling on the floor, heads lowered, looking at the manger scene. Milly put her head close to Kailynn's. "Mommy is seeing Jesus, and someday I will see Him too, and I'll see Mommy."

Kailynn couldn't suppress the tears this time. They filled her eyes to the brim and silently overflowed. "It's so wonderful, Milly, to have Jesus in your heart, and to know He is with you now and forever."

She climbed the stairs of the tri-level home with Milly to the pale pink bedroom with the small pink tea roses on wallpapered borders. There, she brushed the little girl's hair; read her the Bible story about Rebekah from the book on the night stand; and prayed a short prayer with her. She hugged the little girl goodnight before switching off the lamp and closing the door.

Kailynn looked in on Taylor to see that he was still playing a game on his Xbox. She started to tell him to go to bed, but something about the tilt of his head and the defenseless back of his neck persuaded her to give him more time. Since there wasn't any school this week, she could check on him later. In an hour, she observed he had fallen asleep with a book in his hands on top of the covers.

A black Labrador raised his head off the floor at the foot of the bed, lowering it again when he sensed she was harmless. She took a quilt from the back of a nearby chair and spread it across the boy suddenly recognizing it as the red and brown quilt in the DVD. She prayed for him as she turned off the ceiling light and closed the door.

The telephone rang as she entered the guest room downstairs. She hesitated, wondering who would be calling tonight. She picked it up timidly. "Hello?"

"Kailynn?"

Her heart skipped a beat at the sound of the familiar accent. Of course, he would call to check on the children. "Yes, Mr. Webster."

"Please call me Rod. I want to be on a first name basis with anyone who is watching over my kids."

"Okay, Rod. They're both asleep now, but it took Taylor a while to settle down."

"Yeah, he's been like that for some time." There was a pause on his end of the line. "How was your evening?"

"It went fine." Now she paused. "How was your trip?"

"Okay, but I wanted to hear a friendly voice once I arrived. It's been a long time since I've left the children for a business trip."

"I'll do whatever I can to make the days pass quickly for them until you're back home."

"I thought you would, and I know they're fine. I'll try to call earlier tomorrow evening to talk with them." His voice paused again. "Goodnight, Kailynn."

"Goodnight, Mr. Webster…Rod."

She replaced the phone in its base as slowly as she had first picked it up. When it rang again, she hurriedly picked it up, thinking Rod had forgotten to tell her something, but just as she said hello the line went dead. *Maybe he changed his mind or decided to wait until tomorrow.* The caller ID stated UNKNOWN, and she dismissed the call altogether.

Prepared for bed, she didn't expect to sleep much the first night; yet, as soon as she pulled the flowered comforter over her and laid her head on the soft pillows, she began to pray drowsily and finally to fall into a sound sleep.

The sunlight filtered through the sheer curtains and fell across the bed. Waking, she caught a movement in a nearby rocker. On a cushion lay a slender fawn colored cat who opened its big golden eyes, peering in her direction, before curling up tighter into a ball. Having made her bed, showered and dressed in a gray skirt and red sweater, she reached for the doorknob and heard staccato clicking on the linoleum in the kitchen.

Taylor was taking the Lab out the back door when she entered the room. When the dog stopped to look back at Kailynn the boy commanded, "Come on, Stewart, let's go!"

She watched him from the window over the sink. He stopped after a while and stood gazing up at the knoll she had seen in the home movie. She could only imagine his thoughts and his memories. Her heart ached, but she was determined to make this a good day with memories of its own. She fried bacon as perfectly as she could, whisked eggs, adding milk and melted butter in a large plastic measuring cup and scrambled them in an iron skillet. The results were fluffy scrambled eggs with crisp bacon and hot buttered toast when Taylor returned.

Milly, although it was a little chilly, had dressed in flowered pink capris and matching short sleeved sweater and came running into the room, her pony tail flying behind her.

"Yum, what smells so good, Kailynn? Did you make hot chocolate, too?"

"Milly!" Taylor admonished.

"Yes, I did make hot cocoa for you and Taylor, but I'm drinking coffee to wake me up."

"Coffee's not good for you." Again Taylor was attempting to reprimand.

"Too much of anything is not good for anyone." Kailynn was determined to remain cheerful. She said a blessing and prayed mostly for Rod.

"What do you usually have for breakfast?" She asked conversationally.

"We usually have a vitamin packed cereal and orange juice with added calcium and Vitamin C to fight germs in the winter," Taylor informed her in a professional tone.

"That sounds nutritious. What food do you like best?" She held her ground to keep the conversation rolling along.

Milly's eyes widened and she grinned. "Pancakes! With lots of syrup!"

"I like that menu, Milly. Let's talk about what we're going to do today."

"I usually run the sweeper and Milly dusts," Taylor said with the enthusiasm of a wet mop.

"Suppose we do those and other chores, and then make a homemade wreath?" Kailynn suggested.

Both children chimed in unison, "A wreath! How?"

Kailynn leaned forward across the table, and said in jest, "Very carefully."

Milly dusted. Taylor vacuumed. Singing carols, Kailynn loaded the dishwasher and washed the skillet. She knew she didn't sing well, but she sang with her heart; and the work seemed more enjoyable with the effort. Making the beds upstairs, the top floor caught her attention. It had only one door which was locked, and peaked Kailynn's curiosity.

Milly found her sitting at the top of the stairs looking at the door. "Hey, Kailynn, do you want to clean that room?"

"I don't know. Is it an attic or rooms for storage?"

"No. It's Daddy's studio. He used to like to go in there to paint. He keeps the key on the mantle behind one of the vases." Milly started down the stairs. "Do you want to go in there?"

Kailynn hesitated. "Not right now. Maybe later."

The three of them went in search of items she told the children they would need. Taylor found chicken wire out back of the house which they fashioned into a large, fat circle. They wove clippings from the Christmas tree in and out of the holes in the wire. Taylor had a sudden idea, and ran to snip twigs from their holly trees lining the walk at the side patio doors.

"We need to spray this wreath before we decorate it. What can we use here?" Kailynn asked.

Taylor thought for a minute. "I'll search the basement."

When they left it to dry they ate hot dogs for lunch, having thanked God for all the things they had found, drinking Taylor's before mentioned orange juice.

She and Milly found little bells and small bows among the unused ornaments; and Taylor ran upstairs, bringing down miniature sleighs and a couple of tiny red train engines which he declared he no longer needed.

"We'll work them in," Kailynn commented with a smile.

They laughed approvingly as they hung their wreath on the front door.

"Wait 'til Dad gets a load of this!!" Taylor laughed out loud again.

~ ~ ~

After roast beef with potato wedges, onions and carrots baked around it and a cup of Milly's favorite hot chocolate, Kailynn found herself alone again for the rest of the night. Taylor, having walked Stewart, took a shower and settled down with his computer; and Milly fell right to sleep in her bed after a long bubble bath. Still, she felt they had made progress of some kind, and she thanked God.

Soft fur brushed against her leg before Lady, their cat, leaped gracefully into Kailynn's lap, her golden eyes mirroring the satisfaction she felt. She listened to the feline's purr as she stroked the slender body. The telephone rang, but apparently Taylor answered it. Through the vent she heard the words "Dad" and "promise". When he was silent for a long time she realized the conversation had ended. She was inexplicably disappointed that Rod had not asked to speak to her. She picked up her Bible from the end table and started reading the Psalms.

The smell of sausage and pancakes woke both children the next morning, and she could hear them moving around upstairs making their beds as they had promised yesterday. She understood the need for order when there were major problems that seemed beyond your control. For her, order and a sudden need to take action on any decision she could make was a comfort in the past. Why then did she now walk on eggs when coping with adults? With the children she could be herself, part of that true self was a child eager to experience the activities and adventures so many people take for granted.

When they came downstairs, Milly was wearing a long flowered top and black leggings and Taylor a long-sleeved tee shirt and track pants.

Standing in front of the refrigerator, Kailynn waved a carton. "We'll have orange juice this morning since cocoa might be too sweet with pancake syrup." She noticed the children were pleased and ready to thank God.

"You have a nice piano here. Who plays?" She asked conversationally.

The children slowed their eating and looked at each other.

"Mom played," Taylor stated.

"She was giving us lessons," Milly intoned sadly. "I played better than Taylor, but he sang better than me."

Kailynn tried to change the subject to the present. "It's wonderful, Taylor, that you sing."

"Mom said I don't have the range yet that Dad has…had…but when my voice finishes changing I should, but we haven't been singing since… Anyway, I don't know what my range is now."

Kailynn fought the ridiculous temptation to turn in her skipping heart at the nearest drive through hospital. "Why don't we find out when we get the morning chores out of the way? I really don't sing well alone, but I love to try to blend my voice when others sing. Will you help me?"

"Who will play the piano?" Milly asked hopefully.

"Why don't you play? Can you sing when you play?" Kailynn asked.

Milly nodded.

"Taylor, will you and Milly help me pick out some Christmas carols?"

"I guess."

She was unprepared for the music and the voices these children exhibited. At first, they were timid. When they saw the amazed look on her face, they performed, finding comfort in expressing their hearts in the old familiar carols. Emma had taught her children well; and in teaching them, had bestowed upon them a gift that would always comfort them and bring joy to others.

When they took a break for lunch the leftover roast made a delicious vegetable soup. As they enjoyed the warmth of the tasty meal, they discussed the history of some of the carols and the composers. In the afternoon two of Taylor's neighborhood friends came to the door and begged him to shoot basketball with them, and Milly chose to play dolls in her playhouse which her father had brought into the basement for the winter.

The children occupied, Kailynn took the opportunity to search the mantel for the key to the studio. Finding it, she wrestled a few minutes with her intention of entering the room, perhaps to see if it needed cleaning, and Rod's possible reasons for locking the room. If the children knew where to locate the key, why did he lock the door in the first place? Really, she told herself, what harm could there be in her dusting in there?

On opening the door, she saw one large room with a skylight and wide windows. Apparently, the house was built with this studio in mind. Canvases lined the walls. Tables held jars of brushes of various sizes and cases of oil paints. Besides the high stool and an easel, pictures done in charcoal and pastels on a low table near a settee with cushions suggested that Rod sat with his art pad propped against his legs at times. A stack of praise CDs set beside a player. Most of the paintings she could see without moving canvases were of flowers, fields, butterflies and birds. Rod's fascination with colors in nature was obvious. Every painting radiated intricate design indicating the existence of the great Creator of the universe. *Rod is a man who God gifted in many areas of life; and he has used those gifts to glorify Him*, she thought.

Kailynn ran her fingers lightly over the pastels thinking of his hands touching them, working with them to capture nature's beauty in lovely, poignant pictures. She sat down on the end of the settee, her mind troubled. *I might as well say it, Lord,* she silently prayed. *You already know the question pounding my brain. I don't understand why Rod would suffer such a devastating loss in a tragic accident, paralyzing talents honoring You. I don't doubt You care. I don't even doubt You still have a plan, but for me to pretend I understand is hypocrisy. I know this world is in a fallen state of sinful disobedience and continues its physical birth to death cycle with its moral decline. It just hurts so much to meet somebody like Rod who has accepted the salvation You offered through the blood of Your son on the cross, and actually bears witness to Your love as Creator and Your plan of salvation. It is heartbreaking that he was expressing faith through his voice, art, business and family life, and now is seemingly defeated in the prime of his life. All I can say, all I can do, is to pray for You to help him. Please help him, Lord. Help him to understand, help him to rise out of this present darkness into the light of Your love. Help him, Father God, to experience joy again in Jesus' name!*

Meeting in the living room, the children and she decided to shower and change clothes before dinner; and she was glad she was wearing a simple blue dress, and Milly and Taylor were wearing fresh tee shirts and jeans when the front doorbell rang.

"Pizza!" A male voice boomed.

"I'm sorry, but we didn't order pizza," she said to the delivery man with two pizza boxes hiding his head.

Joey's face peeked around the boxes. "Hope you didn't have plans for dinner."

She replied, "I did, but it will keep until tomorrow. Come in."

The children practically jumped at the chance to carry the boxes into the kitchen, and shouted, "Pizza!!"

They were all busy eating and talking about the book store when there was a knock at the back door. Surprised, Kailynn drew the little white curtain aside before opening the door. Agnes Naylor stood there, still a little disheveled from her bout with the flu.

"Oh no, I can see I'm just in time with this warm, homemade chicken soup. Poor Rod. He worries so much about his little children and whether or not they eat when he's gone." She took a deep breath and coughed. "The dear man was smart enough to call me asking about my health, but I know he wanted me to check on Milly and Taylor."

Joey jumped up to take the pan from his sister's hands. "Now, Agnes, you'd better run along home before you make yourself worse, and share more than soup with these kids."

"Thank you, Joey. See to it these children eat more than pizza."

"The pizza is warm, Sis, and loaded with great toppings. Here, let me wrap up a piece for you to take home."

"If you insist, Joey. You're just being polite as always."

"Thank you, Sis."

"Thank you for the soup," Kailynn offered, but the door closed on the last word, and Agnes was gone as quickly as she had come.

After that disturbing visit, she didn't feel like entertaining visitors. Had Rod called Agnes instead of her to check on the children's welfare? Why did he leave her with them if he doubted her ability to care for them?

Sensing her sudden preoccupation, Joey tried to lighten the mood. "Don't pay any attention to my sister. She always likes to stir things up a bit." His face shone with another one of his ideas. "Rod usually takes the children to church at least one night through the week.

Since I'm singing in a quartet tomorrow night at their church, why don't I pick you three up? It would do everybody good to get out a little."

"Quartet? Do you sing with The Shepherd's Men?"

"I sure do."

"You're the tenor!"

"How'd you know?"

"I've attended a lot of praise concerts. That's one thing I *could* do-" She stopped abruptly when he looked puzzled. "We'd love to go. Wouldn't we, Kids?"

They nodded agreement, too busy eating pizza to talk.

Curled up on the sofa alone with her Bible again after Joey left, she answered the phone absentmindedly.

"Kailynn," Rod's voice made her heart leap, but then she remembered his call to Agnes. "How's everything going there?"

"Taylor is asleep early for a change, but Milly just walked into the room." She handed the telephone to his little girl already dressed in her nightgown. "Honey, it's your dad."

"Daddy! I'm glad you called. When are you coming home?" She listened attentively. "That's all right. I'm having a good time. We made a wreath for the front door and sang Christmas carols. And Joey brought us pizza tonight. I'll tell you more when you come home. I love you." For a minute she thought she had been disconnected. "Daddy! I love you."

Kailynn knew by her expression he had finally said, "I love you, too, Pumpkin." She had heard him say it many times over the phone at the shop. She wondered if Milly was too excited to sleep now. She was Daddy's girl.

"Are you doing your devotions?" Milly asked.

"Yes, Sweetheart."

The little girl pulled out a book from the bookcase. At first glance, it appeared to be a black bible. Upon closer examination it turned out to be a devotional. "This was Mommy's book. You may read it if you want sometimes with your Bible.

Kailynn noticed personal notes written throughout the pages. "Honey, your Dad might not want anyone to use this special book."

"He would want you to read it. I know daddy." She yawned, "Goodnight, Kailynn." She planted a light kiss on her babysitter's cheek.

Kailynn sat there, when Milly had gone to bed, with her hands resting on the precious book, looking up at the portrait with the warm, loving face. Great compassion for these children stirred in her heart.

CHAPTER FIVE

Dressed in a basic black dress with only her gold cross with its tiny diamond chip in its center hanging from a delicate chain, Kailynn pulled her hair back at the sides with gold-colored barrettes. Studying her reflection in the dresser mirror she decided to leave the auburn hair cascading in layers onto her shoulders. The barrettes caught the lamp light and sparkled in the mirror. Her eyes glittered dark green, and she glimpsed her small maroon Bible with its little gold clasp also glistening in the reflection and she blushed. "Okay, Lord, I thank You for your love and healing. Help me to live so that Your name is honored."

Each of them was excited about accompanying Joey to church. Milly was dressed in a long royal blue dress and black boots; and once snug in her hooded coat, also blue, practically danced with excitement. Taylor insisted on wearing jeans, but his sweater was a thick knitted burgundy. He, too, was glad when Joey rang the front doorbell though he tried to conceal his own enthusiasm. Joey, handsome in a gray suit and overcoat, held Kailynn's black winter coat as she slipped her arms into it. They all agreed to walk the short distance to the church. Fat snowflakes floated around them as they left the house.

The sanctuary in the neat brick church reminded Kailynn of her version of an ark. The sides of the room shone of wood, one aisle divided the polished pews on either side. Behind the podium a large cross glowed like a beacon beckoning souls to surrender to the Savior who loved them enough to sacrifice Himself upon Calvary and rise again to save them from a death sentence, and offer them eternal life. *If only they accept the offer,* she thought. The sound system surrounded the sanctuary with music. The quartet harmonized beautifully and, at times, above the voices the tenor's soared. They sang of the beauty of creation, walking daily with God, sailing through the storms of life, earthly sunsets, heaven's gates and streets pure as gold. When their songs were ended, many members said they felt they had taken a trip and returned refreshed.

Walking home through the snow whitening the streets and lawns, Joey, Kailynn and the children sang

Christmas carols. Inside the house, they made hot chocolate, popped popcorn and played a board game.

Kailynn waited until Joey had left before suggesting the children go to bed. Settled down in the living room with Emma's devotional on her lap, she was startled when Taylor appeared in front of her.

"I thought you might like to hear this CD since you seemed to like the singing tonight."

Curious, she extended a hand for the disc; but he paused before letting it go.

"It's Dad's voice…the way he used to sing. People say his songs comfort them. Sometimes, I play it in my room when he's gone or when I'm sure he won't hear."

"Thank you, Taylor. I'd like very much to hear his voice."

"The player is in that cabinet in the entertainment center. Just pull the door open and leave it." Without another word, he walked upstairs.

A rich baritone voice filled the room. Rod sang about Christ being the anchor through troubled times. His voice soothed, and then penetrated her soul. She felt strength flow into her spirit and a resolve before God to hold fast to that anchor, and make it through all the uncertainties to the city of God.

The incessant ringing of the telephone penetrated Kailynn's contemplation.

"Hello."

"Were you asleep already?" It was Rod's voice softened with its slight defect.

"No, far from it."

"You sound like you had a good day."

"Yes, I did, and a wonderful evening. We went to your church with Joey where he sang tonight."

The line went silent so long she began to think he had hung up.

"Hello?"

"I'm here. I'm sorry, I guess I'm tired. I'll call back to talk with the children earlier tomorrow evening when I feel fresher. Have a good night, Kailynn."

"You too, Rod. Goodnight." She felt disappointed again that they had spoken so little. *I can't call him back. He said he was tired and it would be rude if not impertinent unless there was an emergency.* She mused for a few minutes before telling herself, *There is something I can do. I can pray for him.*

The telephone rang, and she answered with a hopeful hello. There was no reply. Someone was on the line, but remained silent. She examined the device and noticed the word UNKNOWN again. She shrugged her shoulders as she placed the phone in its base. When the phone rang again she hesitated, but noticing Nadine's name, she finally picked it up.

"Hello?"

"Hello! Is Rod there?"

"No, I'm sorry, but he is out of town. Would you like to leave a message?"

"No... I'm his sister-in-law. Just calling to chat a little. May I ask who you are?"

"Oh, Nadine, this is Kailynn. I'm staying with the children while Rod attends a conference."

"That's nice of you, Kailynn. Hope he gets home before the weather gets too bad. The snow is really coming down here. Well, I'll let you get some rest." Nadine's voice rose in laughter. "Knowing my niece and nephew, you probably will need it!"

Kailynn laughed, too. "You're right about that. My mind is working on ideas to keep them busy and entertained so they don't miss their dad too much. Try to stay warm and have a good night."

"You, too, Kailynn. Good Night."

The phone was hardly back on the base when it rang again. "Hello…"

"Kailynn?" Agnes' voice was hoarse, but she recognized it. "Are the children settled in for the night?"

"Yes, they are." Kailynn tried to make her voice sound reassuring. "I'm getting ready to settle down, myself."

"Okay. I'm just checking on them before I take my cough medicine. It makes me drowsy." She coughed into the receiver. "I'll call tomorrow when I feel up to it."

"You do that, Agnes. Hope you feel better soon."

The line went dead.

She opened the little devotional. "The Kingdom of God is within you" was underlined. With faith, believing, she prayed earnestly for Rod, and one by one for the children, Joey, her parents, Carla now heavy with child, Carla's husband, Sara and yes, even Agnes Naylor.

~ ~ ~

She woke with a start, realizing morning had dawned and she had slept in the chair. She hurried to the bedroom to prepare for the day.

When the three had bundled up in heavy jeans, jackets, scarves and toboggans later in the morning, they ascended the hill behind the house, leaving footprints in the snow. Together they packed and rolled large balls of snow, and built a huge snowman giving him black button eyes and a carrot nose. When Taylor went to the house for a scarf and toboggan for their new friend he returned with a sled. They took turns sliding down a slope.

Kailynn, with a racing heart, laughed, thrilled by her scary descent and occasional upset in snow drifts while fending off Stewart who was barking gleefully and trying to keep her down. She had never had so much fun in her life; and the children laughed, overjoyed by her delight.

Happily breathless, they started for the house when passing their snowman, Kailynn asked, "You know what our new friend here needs?"

The children looked critically at the snowman, and not detecting anything missing, they shook their heads.

"Well, he looks lonely out here all by himself. I think he needs a dog."

"A dog!" Their young voices exclaimed, and their eyes looked disbelieving in her direction before turning their focus to Stewart and back again to Kailynn's face. Stewart recognized the word dog and wagged his tail, but since everyone stood stock still he cocked his head in curiosity.

"I don't mean Stewart," she laughed. "Let's make a dog for Frosty!"

"It would be easier to make him a Mrs. Frosty than to make a dog," Taylor suggested.

"How?" his sister asked. "How do we make a dog?"

Kailynn bent and scooped snow into both gloved hands. "The same way we made the snowman, except we will have to put legs on him, ears and a tail. He can be a white poodle sitting up."

They watched her roll a snowball into the bulk of the body, and a smaller one for the head. Catching on to the canine image she had in her mind, they each took a part they wanted to sculpt onto the form. Digging down through the snow they found pebbles they used for the eyes and nose. Stepping back to take in the scene of the snowman and his snow-dog, they felt pleased.

"Wait here. Gotta get a picture of them!" Taylor ran toward the house to fetch his cell phone.

On his return, Kailynn insisted on taking the picture with the two kids standing on either side of their creations.

She arose earlier the next day to read more of Emma's devotional and to pray. As she picked up the book it fell open to a scripture verse which her spirit sensed was a literal warning to her. 1 Peter 4:12-13 "Beloved, think it not strange concerning the fiery trial which is to try you, as though some strange thing happened unto you: But rejoice, inasmuch as ye are partakers of Christ's suffering; that, when His glory shall be revealed, ye may be glad also with exceeding joy." She felt an urge to print it on a card. Again, as she leafed through the pages, scripture leaped out at her. Ephesians 6:12-18 "For we wrestle not against flesh and blood, but against principalities, against powers, against the rulers of the darkness of this world, against spiritual wickedness in high places. Wherefore take unto you the whole armor of God, that ye may be able to withstand in the evil day, and having done all, to stand. Stand therefore, having your loins girt about with truth, and having on the breastplate of righteousness; And your feet shod with the preparation of the gospel of peace; Above all, taking the shield of faith, wherewith ye shall be able to quench all the fiery darts of the wicked. And take the helmet of salvation, and the sword of the Spirit, which is the word of God: Praying always with all prayer and supplication in the Spirit, and watching thereunto with all perseverance and supplication for all saints."

She knew she had received important instructions from a manual designed to see Christians through spiritual warfare, and memorized them. Gratitude for the word of God enveloped her as she worshiped Him in praise.

After a breakfast of hot oatmeal sweetened with a touch of cinnamon, she asked the children to gather up all the soiled clothes and she would sort them into baskets to wash. Having emptied hampers in bathrooms and bedrooms while picking up scattered socks in their rooms, the children bundled up and set out with their dog to play with their neighborhood friends.

Kailynn hadn't realized there would be so many clothes and towels or she would have sorted them in the basement. She was busy in the middle of this disarray, wearing her long denim skirt and matching blouse, when someone knocked at the back door. Thinking it was one of the children with their dog, she opened the door. Standing there in mock surprise was Agnes Naylor practically covered with black earmuffs, toboggan, slacks, boots and a long black jacket.

"I see my presence is definitely needed in this home. Just give me a few minutes to hang up my things. We don't need more clothes littering the house, do we?"

"That's all right, Agnes, I have it under control," she said, all the while reminding herself that "we wrestle not against flesh and blood…"

Agnes didn't seem to hear as she headed toward the coat closet in the living room. Kailynn stood her ground behind her. "Sorry, Agnes, I would rather sort the clothes myself. You're welcome to eat chili with us at lunchtime though." She handed Agnes her coat.

Angry, Agnes grabbed her earmuffs and toboggan. "No, thank you. I really don't need another upset stomach on top of everything else." She marched out the front door, leaving it for Kailynn to close.

Kailynn sighed in relief. In the basement, she put on a Christian radio station waiting to talk to God about her encounter with Agnes and the entire situation. She no longer felt alone. She felt surrounded by God's love and heavenly host.

The clothes folded, she carried baskets one at a time up to the dining room between the kitchen and the living room stairs. Stirring the chili the children had begged her to prepare, she looked out the window, but didn't see them.

The front doorbell rang, and she momentarily expected them to shake snow through the living room when she opened the door. She recognized the man, however, as soon as she stood face to face. He was older than she had surmised earlier. His lean physique lent to the youthful illusion. It was the man who tried to help the night of the accident. He was holding a stack of wrapped presents against his blue jacket. His dark eyes crinkled at the corners in recognition also. "Well, howdy, Miss! This is a surprise."

Kailynn smiled weakly and stepped aside to let him enter. "Won't you come in?"

"I don't want to track snow into the room, but if you would put these gifts under the tree I'd appreciate it." As she took the presents, he ran a hand over his straight dark hair slicking it back. "Where are the kids? I've been checking on them and their dad ever since the accident. That was the least I could do. I guess you had the same idea."

"I came to know them through the book store. I work there…at least for now. Rod is out of town, but the children are playing outside. They should be here for lunch. Would you care for a cup of coffee?"

"Sounds good, but I have one more gift to deliver to Agnes next door." In answer to Kailynn's upraised eyebrows he explained., "The children stayed at her place while their parents made a trip to a country church where her brother sang the night of the accident."

Kailynn tensed. *Lord, this is a strange way to answer my prayers.* Immediately the phrase popped into her mind, *"God works in mysterious ways…"*

He offered a hand. "I'm sorry. I never introduced myself. I'm Rudy L. Gordon. Friends call me R.L. I'm glad to see you here."

Balancing the packages, she stuck out her hand enough to shake his hand with her fingers. "I'm Kailynn Richardson. It's nice of you to keep in touch with the family. I'm sure your visits helped them to cope with their loss."

"They mean a lot to me, now. Well, have a merry Christmas, and I hope to see you again."

"Thank you."

Her mind spinning, she placed the gifts under the tree. Still wondering where the children were, she looked out the kitchen window, noticing the blazer parked in front of Agnes' two story white house.

She had decided to put on her jacket and trudge through the snow when she saw the vehicle pull away. The children were walking down the sidewalk from Agnes' house.

"Hey, Kailynn, where are you going?" Taylor yelled.

Suddenly annoyed, she answered, "Looking for you."

"Agnes asked us to come eat tomato soup and cheese sandwiches with her. She said you wouldn't mind." Taylor waited, observing her reaction.

Milly exclaimed happily, "R.L. said he left gifts for us. I can't wait to see the packages!"

Kailynn's heart melted at the sight of Milly's face. R.L. must not have mentioned her involvement. She wanted a chance to explain everything to Rod when he returned.

The Christmas lights blinked as the skies darkened and snow began falling again.

~   ~   ~

Taylor could not eat enough chili for supper, and drank about a quart of milk. She wondered if his hunger for it was because he played so long in the snow, building an appetite, if he liked the taste of the chili that much, or if he was trying to make up for the misunderstanding at lunchtime. She finally deduced that all three reasons were valid conclusions.

She heard her bedroom door open in the middle of the night and sat bolt upright, turning on the lamp. Milly, in a white gown, squeezed apologetically through the doorway. "Kailynn," she said sleepily,. "Could I take Lady to my bed? It's lonely in my room. Daddy has been gone for days and he didn't even call this evening. Do you think he's all right? What if something happened to Daddy?"

Kailynn reached for her terrycloth robe at the foot of the bed. Lady was lying on the corner, her slender tail wrapped around her back legs. She patted the bed beside her and Milly curled up. "Oh, Honey, he's probably fine. Just busy and tired. More than likely he fell asleep. Did you pray for him?"

"Yes. I asked God to watch over him and keep him safe."

"Did you believe God could do that?"

"Oh, yes, Kailynn. He can hear me and I know He can do that. Can I ask you something personal?"

"OK."

"Why do you have a scar on your chest? Did you fall down and cut yourself?'

Pulling the robe over her gown, she tied it tightly together. "No, Honey. I had to have an operation."

Milly's brown eyes penetrated her blue-green ones wonderingly. "What kind of operation?"

"Well, actually, the doctors had to fix my heart. Mine wasn't working too well...so they operated to make it work better."

"A good heart?"

"Yes, a good heart."

"My mother had a good heart. Everybody was always saying she had a good heart."

"I'm sure she did, Sweetheart."

The little girl dozed against her sitter's shoulder. Kailynn waited for a few precious minutes before waking her just enough to lead her back upstairs to her own bed. Love overwhelmed her as she tucked the cover up around the little girl's shoulders. She then carried the slender fawn-furred cat in her arms up to Milly's bed, and closed the bedroom door. If the child woke again through the night, Lady would be there with her calm golden eyes to comfort her.

After soaking in warm bath water to soothe her muscles, hoping to induce sleep again, Kailynn slipped into a long, loose gold-colored dress she had often found comfortable enough to lull herself to sleep at home. The soft material always made her feel cozy. She wrapped a white towel like a turban around her head. She carried a cup of steaming herbal tea from the kitchen to the fireplace in the living room. She smiled thinking about Taylor taking the fireplace as his responsibility. He added wood before going to bed and took care of the fire first thing every morning while Rod was gone. He said it kept the downstairs warm, and saved energy not to mention money for his Dad. The heat from the flames began to warm her, and she sat on the sofa drying her hair.

The sound of a motor caught her attention as a vehicle slowly pulled into the drive. A car door slammed shut. She rose with the intention of peeking through the draperies when the lights went out. Slits of light filtered around windows with brightness of the snow as her eyes adjusted. Her ears could hear stomping and scraping as someone tried the doorknob and then pushed against the door. Stewart was suddenly by her side, his body taut in expectation. She picked up a vase about the time someone fiddled with the lock and pushed their way into the room. She gave a breathless scream as she reared back to throw the glassware.

"Whoa! Kailynn!" Rod's voice exclaimed as loudly as he could muster seeing her in the firelight, poised for attack.

Stewart's tail wagged as he pranced around his master.

She hugged the vase to her throat as she exhaled in relief. "I wasn't expecting anyone."

"Sorry I didn't call. Heard about the snowstorm hitting and was afraid I couldn't get back for a while. Drove straight through. Had a hard time seeing the road. And the heater quit on me halfway here." He took a breath and looked at her thoughtfully. "Didn't mean to scare you. Had a hard time getting my key to work."

She noticed the red hands he held up even in the dim light. "You must be frozen. Take your wet coat off and sit in front of the fireplace. Do you think I could warm chili over the fire?"

"Sure. Bring the pot holders. A long-handled pan is hanging with others above the stove. Candles are on the dining room table and matches in the kitchen cabinet, top shelf."

As she lit the candles, she determined to tell Rod all about her presence the night of the accident.

The chili barely heated, she encouraged him to eat from the pan with the ladle. "The chili powder and onions will warm you and, believe it or not, the chili might seem to taste better that way."

Rod was starting to feel comfortable in his bulky amber sweater over a shirt. "You're right. My throat feels better already."

Stewart, content now that his master was home, laid his head on Rod's shoes.

Kailynn noticed Rod's noble forehead again and the way one strand of blond hair which had so far escaped the silver fell across it. "Are you finished already?"

"Full and satisfied. Thank you, Kailynn." He placed the pan on the hearth and sat back on the sofa, stretching one arm over the back.

"I have something to explain, Rod."

"You don't need to explain. I should have called instead of bursting in unexpectedly. I thought everyone would be asleep." He paused and reached out his fingers to touch her hair. "Your hair is damp." The red highlights shone in firelight. Her smooth complexion looked ivory in the candlelight though her cheekbones suddenly flushed. Her eyes, now green, sparkled darkly as they met his blue piercing inspection. Their gaze switched on its own strong connection as the lamps suddenly lit the room.

"Let me…let me make you a hot cup of herbal tea, too. It will help you catch up on sleep." She rose as if escaping an awkward situation when the truth was she really would have liked the two of them to sit like that for a very long time. She knew instinctively that particular moment would live forever in her memory.

When she returned with the tea, she found him sleeping on the sofa. She set the mug down on a coaster on the coffee table and covered him with the afghan no doubt crocheted by his beloved wife. She stood looking down at this man wondering how she could tell him her version of that night.

She squelched a longing to grow close to him. How could she ever measure up to the wonderful wife and mother Emma had obviously been? She picked up the towel from the arm of the couch and blew the candles out. Saddened, she walked slowly into her room and locked the door with a click of finality.

CHAPTER SIX

The brightness of the sun glancing off the snow through the sheer curtains invaded her sleepy eyelids. She woke in spite of herself to the sound of joyous voices downstairs. Her head still resting on her pillow, she stretched and smiled at the image of Milly dancing around her father, loneliness forgotten at the appearance of him asleep in the living room instead of his bedroom.

She splashed cold water onto her face even before showering, and brushed her teeth until her gums tingled with that fresh taste of mint toothpaste. Choosing dark blue jeans and matching turtleneck sweater, she hoped for one more romp in the snow with the children before going home. She fried bacon and folded omelets this morning for breakfast. She wanted to have more time with the kids, though Rod could hardly get away from them long enough to take a shower in his private bathroom. He came to the kitchen table, freshly shaved, also wearing jeans with a bulky maroon sweater. They were all dressed with the same idea of enjoying the snow.

The children talked animatedly about the snowman they had already built; and they and their father planned the clothes they would take in a backpack for the second one.

"You should see Kailynn slide down the hill, Dad!" Taylor interjected.

"I intend to see her slide down that hill. Does she use a sled?" They all laughed happily at this question.

Rod put out a gloved hand to help Kailynn up the hill. She grasped his glove with her own as best she could though she felt energetic enough to fly without anyone's help. She was sure that feeling was exhilaration more than anything. The children worked together, rolling part of the snowman while she and Rod worked on another section. This time they dressed their new creation in a vest, and he looked very dignified for a snowman.

The children slid down the slope one at a time. Rod slid with Milly a couple of times. Stewart was again ready to accompany Kailynn's spills into the snow with his ecstatic barks. Laughter and barking brought Agnes Naylor, dressed in a striped robe out on her back porch.

After she stood for a few moments staring grimly, she grabbed a broom and began to furiously sweep the snow off the steps.

Back inside the kitchen, having hung their jackets up to dry, they sipped hot chocolate.

"Would you kids please put your clean clothes away before I leave?"

"You're going home today?" Milly seemed to have taken it for granted that she would stay through the weekend. "She doesn't have to leave...Does she, Daddy? Just because you're home."

"No, Kailynn, you don't have to leave. You could go to church with us Sunday," Rod offered.

"I'd better spend a little time with my folks before going back to work," she replied truthfully.

"Will you come hear me sing at the church with my class on Christmas Eve?" Milly begged, as if she had to exact a promise of Kailynn's continued presence in her life before letting her go home.

"As a matter of fact," Rod joined in, "I'm in the play. I'd like you to spend Christmas Eve and Christmas Day with us."

"Well, Christmas Eve is fine, but Christmas Day..." she began.

"Now, don't say your parents can't do without you. We'd like to invite them too. It would be nice to have your family here to help us celebrate the birth of Christ," Rod suggested.

"Come on, Kailynn," Taylor urged.

"Please..." Milly's eyes pleaded.

"Maybe you have other plans..." Rod thought suddenly before he continued, "with other people."

Kailynn, who had been looking from one child's face to the other, looked straight into his penetrating eyes.

"No, I don't have plans. It would be fun for my family to celebrate with the kids." To change the subject and the focus of his attention, she asked, "Who do you portray in the play?"

"It's a silent part. I'm one of the three wise men."

"The wisest and the best," Milly proclaimed.

Kailynn was glad to be back in her family's comfortable cottage - an oddity amidst St. Albans tall old houses - and her childhood room with its white tie-back curtains and familiar pictures of her mother and father taken at church for the directory. Her bedroom furniture was painted a light blue reminding her of frosting on a few of her birthday cakes. The fairy-tale figures of Cinderella and Snow White had been replaced by ceramic pink roses.

She was thankful for the simplicity of her girlhood home to think about the week she had just experienced, to assess her situation and in time to come to a sensible decision with God's help to reveal her knowledge of their past ordeal. Hopefully, she would still be their friend. More to the truth, that they would be her friends, for they had already won her heart; and she could never blame them if they thought less of her. She wished she could have been as open as R.L. had been with them. Of course, she had been in no condition, herself, to visit them or attend the funeral. They had had no idea the extent of her concern or compassion.

She prayed earnestly for their family during the organ prelude in her own family's church comforted by the fact that its stone edifice had endured the onslaught of time. Afterward, they enjoyed a breaded baked chicken dinner prepared by her mother, bustling around in one of her flowered dresses partially covered by a white apron. Kailynn noticed her offering a bowl of heaping mashed potatoes to her grinning dad as though it were a gift of jewels. And he accepted it as such, love shining in his dark eyes as much as always through the years. Would she ever experience this lasting kind of love? Could she deserve it? She had never learned to do well the tasks good wives seem to do naturally. Her mother did so many wonderful things like sewing clothes for her little girl, waxing floors until they reminded people of mirrors, gardening and canning with her husband so that they ate their vegetables even in winter. Most of the time, the flowers that graced the dining room table were grown by her. *She is a true Proverbs 31 woman,* Kailynn thought.

Now Kailynn wanted to be more like her mother. She understood at last that you want to serve those you love, that you want to see them comfortable and happy.

In the afternoon, she let herself into the closed bookstore. Depending on the brightness of the snow through the plate glass window, she walked contentedly around the book and gift displays. She saw in addition to the usual arrangements, bookcases holding new books. She saw recently installed light strips. Joey and Sara had been busy indeed. She moved through the quietness of the building, running her fingertips across books representing lives and studies until she came to the back office. A figure stood silently in the dimness. As she moved near, their eyes met and held.

"Do you need a ride home?" Roderick whispered.

She nodded a silent yes.

They spoke little during the drive, mostly about the improvements to the store in their absence.

"See you in church," he said as he opened the car door.

"See you," she responded.

The Webster's church was decorated beautifully on Christmas Eve with greenery, wreaths, ribbons and candles. Kailynn, dressed in a long dark green dress, her hair in a twist with small emerald earrings encircled with tiny diamond chips adorning her ears and a delicate pendant to match gracing her slender neck, allowed her parents to enter the pew before seating herself. She felt a little self-conscious because she had taken more time than usual to apply make-up and dress herself carefully. She suddenly felt like a decorated Christmas tree. In reality, she appeared lovely to all those around her; and they smiled with admiration.

Joey, in a charcoal suit, arrived with Agnes who was decked out in red, both shaking hands on their way toward the Richardsons. Kailynn introduced them just as the program started; and Joey sat down beside her, his sister acting congenial on this special occasion on the other side of her brother in the same pew.

The music to *It Came Upon a Midnight Clear* sounded as the children proceeded down the center aisle toward the stage, divided and stepped up from both sides until they gathered in a choir singing "O Little Town of

Bethlehem." Kailynn recognized Milly in the front row, her velvet blue dress touching the tops of her patent leather shoes. Her golden hair cascaded from a blue ribbon sweeping the sides from her temples.

While the choir sang the last verse, Milly walked to the piano to the right. The chorus finished, she began to play "Silent Night" and her voice sang sweetly. The choir joined her for the last verse. Taylor walked over and stood beside the piano; and Kailynn sat almost on the edge of her seat as his deepening voice sang "We Three Kings." The three kings entered the stage left slowly as though traveling from a great distance. The choir dispersed revealing a living manger scene. As two of the wise men picked up the lines "We Three Kings", the third one who was Roderick Webster, in a very realistic costume – at least from a distance - offered his gift of gold first. Kailynn, deliberately putting the knowledge on hold that Baby Jesus lived in a house in Bethlehem when the kings finally found Him, enjoyed the production for its worshipful poignancy. Mary pondered aloud regarding the shepherds and the visit of the three kings. She and Joseph sang *Away In The Manger*. In the end, angels reappeared singing with the music *It Came Upon A Midnight Clear*.   Applause broke out for a good two minutes before everyone on stage bowed and then turned toward the glowing cross above and joined the congregation in applause.

The pastor then expressed his appreciation for everyone involved in the production of the play. Kailynn noted that he gave special thanks to Agnes Naylor for her untiring work on the costumes, and felt humbled beyond measure. Agnes' smile glistened as she showed her perfect teeth.

Later, Kailynn and Joey stepped behind the stage to tell the children and Rod the extent of their enjoyment. Milly hugged her. "Taylor and I were going to back out until we sang at home with you last week, Kailynn. Thank you."

Rod took off the homemade crown and wiped his forehead with a paper towel. He sounded breathless as he shook their hands and said he was glad they had come. As she turned to descend the stage, he called her name still somewhat breathless. "Will you come home with us to have eggnog and cookies with the kids?"

The children looked at her expectantly. "I'd love to. Mother and Dad need to turn in early if they're going to come to dinner tomorrow, but I'll wait in the vestibule.

Joey's eyebrows raised as he stood motionless, one hand on Kailynn's right elbow ready to help her down off the stage.

"Would...would you like to come too, Joey?" Rod asked.

"I promised to help Agnes with some dishes she is preparing for the dinner. We'll see all of you tomorrow."

For a moment, she could hardly hide her surprise, but recovered her composure. Why shouldn't Rod invite his old friends as usual?

Around the table in the kitchen, they talked about the performance and the funny incidents during rehearsals a month ago. Kailynn took pleasure watching Rod's handsome mouth spread in broad smiles and the cleft in his strong chin widen in laughter with his children. She loved seeing Taylor throw his head back in heartfelt laughter like he had laughed during their escapades in the snow. When Milly giggled almost into her plate of cookies and nearly spilled her eggnog a thrill ran through her whole being.

"Oh, this has really been fun, but I better go home so I'll be able to get up a little earlier. Mother may need help," she reluctantly informed them.

"Taylor, can you make sure the two of you get ready for bed? I'm going to drive Kailynn home, but I'll be back within the hour."

"Sure, Dad. See ya tomorrow at dinner, Kailynn."

"I'm looking forward to it. Goodnight."

As they stood, Milly wrapped her arms around Kailynn's waist, and rose on tiptoes to kiss her cheek. "We'll always be friends, won't we?"

"I sure hope so, Sweetheart. Goodnight."

The streets were quiet as Rod and Kailynn drove. The clouds parted, exposing stars twinkling in the night sky. Most homes had left their Christmas lights lit to acknowledge Christmas Eve. It was interesting to see the various decorations – manger scenes, sleighs, reindeer, carolers and many more. It seemed everyone had something unique to exhibit.

As Rod pulled up in front of the Richardson's house, he touched her coat sleeve with his right hand. "Thank you, Kailynn."

She looked at him questioningly. "For what?"

"For everything you've done for the kids."

"I haven't done anything except have fun with them."

"That's what I mean. That's quite a lot." He patted her shoulder.

When he had walked around the car and opened the door for her, she dropped one of her gloves in the snow. He bent to retrieve it. As she took it from him their fingers touched and both seemed to have forgotten the many times they had unloaded boxes of books together or filed papers or passed a cup of hot chocolate. It was as if this contact were the first. All of a sudden they were self-conscious. Without looking at her face again, he walked her to the porch and said a quick goodnight.

~ ~ ~

By morning, Kailynn and her parents were excited with anticipation of joining Rod and his children for a Christmas dinner. Her father, always conservative, appeared as calm as ever, but couldn't keep the light from dancing in his eyes. Both in robes after their warm baths, the two women chatted happily when they worked on each other's hair in Kailynn's room. Holding one dress up, and then another, like a giddy school girl, Mae changed her mind over and over. Going through her jewelry box she picked up a pearl necklace, then a broach, then a choker, and then back to the pearls. As they talked non-stop something suddenly occurred to Kailynn. Her mother noticed the pause in conversation, the change in the atmosphere and her daughter's demeanor.

Mae looked up from her seat in front of the dresser to see a crease forming between her daughter's brows. "Honey, is anything wrong? What is it?"

Kailynn took a deep breath through her nostrils and let it fill her lungs. Exhaling, she felt she needed to tiptoe around her words to avoid hurting her mother's feelings.

"Well?" Mae's pointed tone poked at Kailynn's thoughts.

She sat down on the bed across from her mother. "It's such a happy occasion, Mother, I don't want any reminders of my heart surgery or the accident I witnessed on the ridge. You know how one thing leads to another during dinner conversation. Do you think we could skip bringing up these subjects?"

"Why, yes, Sweetheart, we could. There's no reason we have to spoil this joyous time by relating those difficult days."

When her father opened the door to ask his wife if he should wear a tie, he winked at the two ladies. "What's so serious?"

Mae shrugged her shoulders. "Oh… nothing … really. Kailynn doesn't want us to mention her heart surgery or the tragic accident she witnessed. She thinks it might spoil this joyous occasion."

Lee looked at his daughter, who now stood up quietly waiting for a question and answer session. Instead, Lee replied, "No problem. That kind of talk doesn't belong at a festive dinner table."

Mae grinned. "Well, I will silently thank God for my little girl's successful surgery, and for keeping her safe."

"Mother, I'm not a little girl anymore!"

Laughing, Mae countered, "You will always be my little girl, Kailynn Richardson!"

All smiles, the two women hugged, and were caught up in their preparations again.

The scent of pine needles and holly berry candles mingled with the stuffed turkey Rod had baked, the many vegetables dishes, pumpkin pies and spice cakes Mrs. Richardson and Agnes had brought. Kailynn's favorite was one of her mother's moist fruit cakes. It was rich in taste and calories which was probably why she, Rod and the children were the only people to eat it. Low-fat whipped cream topped the slices of pumpkin pie and spice cake. She brewed more coffee for those who enjoyed it with desert.

At first, she resented the seating arrangements: Rod, casually dressed in a gray sweater, at one end of the dining room table and Agnes, wearing red again at the other end, her smile radiant as she took the role of hostess to the Richardsons. Kailynn's mother and father, wearing last night's dress clothes, sat to Rod's left with Taylor closest to Rod's chair, and she and Joey to the right with Milly near Rod and across the table from her brother. Kailynn admitted to herself that this was probably the most practical arrangement since Joey, attired in a crisp white shirt and dark dress pants, sat near his sister; and she, dressed in her long black skirt and white sweater with the delicate cross dangling over the soft neckline, found herself facing her parents. Agnes had known the family for a long time, she reasoned, probably before her husband died from cancer. If Rod would be interested in any other woman at all as wife and mother, surely it would be natural for him to consider Agnes. This thought didn't please her as much as she was certain it should.

She turned her attention to Joey, engaging in light conversation, discussing amusing happenings in the store while she had been gone, changes in shelving and lighting in the building, Carla in triage in the hospital on Christmas Eve and Sara spending the holidays with her parents and married sister. Out of the corner of her eye, she saw her dad nudge her mother and they smiled approvingly. Agnes beamed and offered a dish of cranberries to Kailynn who felt she'd accept this little gesture of friendship.

While the children talked about their gifts and board games they had discovered under the tree early this morning, Rod stood up. Passing Kailynn's chair, he bent to whisper in her ear. "Could I see you in the kitchen for a few minutes?"

"Sure." As she pushed her chair back to rise, Joey watched quietly.

Agnes, in conversation with Mrs. Richardson, tried to keep her eyes on Rod.

In the kitchen, Rod leaned his back against the sink counter while Kailynn stood waiting in front of him. "I don't know how to ask you this without putting you on the spot. I don't want a positive answer if you would rather do something else. I don't want you to feel intimidated or obliged to agree."

"What in the world is it, Rod?"

"The kids need to come home after school. I don't want them going somewhere else if they don't have to or want to....not yet anyway. Agnes prefers them to come to her house. So much has changed; I don't want their routine disrupted as well."

"I understand," she agreed.

"Say no without fear of offending me or reprisal, Kailynn."

She stood silently considering this offer.

"If I moved your hours up a bit at the store, would you be willing to stay with the kids…just until I get home?"

She backed against the kitchen table, and put out a hand to steady it. "Why me?"

"The kids want you here."

"What do *you* want?"

Off guard, he stretched out his arms on either side and clutched the counter. "I want you…here…." He tightened his lips and then relaxed them in a smile. "…with the children."

Her heart skipped a beat at his disconcerting behavior. "Could I think about it for a little while?"

"Certainly. Take your time. The kids don't have to go back to school until after New Year's Day, and I'm spending most of the week with them."

"Hey Rod," Agnes' voice flowed into the kitchen before she pushed open the door with one hop and carried food dishes in both hands to the table. "Let the youngsters go play board games, while we put away the food and clean up. I've asked Joey to lead us in carols later. Is that alright with you?"

"Good idea, Agnes."

Mrs. Richardson, accustomed to her role as lady of the house on holidays, carried plates into the kitchen. When Kailynn went to the dining room table to help, Joey took a dish out of her hand. "Come on, Girl; let's see the new games the kids received this year."

"Okay. But wait a moment. I have a couple of gifts for them in my bookbag." She had enjoyed thinking of them while she shopped, although her time was limited in selecting the gifts: a really good harmonica for Taylor and sheet music including Franz Lizt's Leiberstraum which she, herself, liked to hear at concerts for Milly along with a couple of books. Unexpectedly, they presented her with a DVD of their performance at the church.

In the evening, they all gathered in front of the living room fireplace for devotions. Joey asked Milly to play the piano and he led everyone in a medley of carols. Agnes, in a festive mood, suggested, "Silver Bells; then, as Milly stepped down from the piano, began singing in a soprano voice which impressed and humbled Kailynn. When all had ended that song, Agnes looked at Rod and sang a line: "walking in the winter wonderland." At once, everyone joined in the song. He stopped trying to sing, however, and gazed across the room at Kailynn realizing that Joey, sitting next to her, was actually singing to her. Before anyone could suggest another song, the telephone rang.

Milly ran to answer it. Handing the cordless phone to her father, she announced importantly, "Carla has a baby boy!"

Rod set the phone on speaker, and everyone joined in to say Congratulations!

Christmas carols were forgotten as the phone rang again. This time it was the children's aunt with their grandparents saying Merry Christmas. Together, Milly and Taylor yelled Merry Christmas into the phone before Rod took the phone back to talk privately with Emma's family.

~ ~ ~

For almost a week, Kailynn didn't see Rod or the children. Business had slowed down after Christmas; and Joey could take the time to train Sara and her on the new computer. He said that every employee should be able to locate merchandise whether or not it was displayed or merely in stock. During this week she delighted in being of service to customers seeking literature on certain subjects, wholesome stories dealing with challenges or art and music to inspire worship. Still, she missed her boss working methodically, conversing carefully with customers, and especially standing at the end of the counter reading the newspaper at the close of the workday. The week was nearly over when Rod called her at the shop.

"Kailynn, how are you?"

"Fine. Sorry I haven't called. I've been trying to catch onto the new software program, besides doing the general work. Why haven't you stopped by whenever you were out?"

"I thought it best to give you and Joey at least a week's break from us for his sake without telling you the reason. But that doesn't seem fair."

"Fair?"

"Yes. Keep quiet about it for now." His voice lowered even more than usual. "Joey came to my house to see me."

"He did?" She was puzzled why this visit would seem unusual to Rod who saw Agnes and Joey frequently. Agnes. Oh no. Was there a discussion about Kailynn? Had R.L. mentioned something to her after all? And did Rod now have Agnes' version of that terrible night? She dared to breathe again.

Rod continued, "I should tell you in person. It's difficult as it is. On the phone it's impossible."

Was he firing her? Whatever, she wanted him to hear her explanation.

"I'm coming over there on my lunch break," she insisted.

"I would pick you up, but right now that might look inappropriate."

"I'll be there in a few minutes."

"Right. Bye."

"Bye," she whispered weakly.

She took off her smock and hung it in the back hall. Straightening her green dress with the gold trim and reaching for her coat, she told Sara who was boxing books for delivery that she was going to take a break. All the way over to Rod's house, she rehearsed her version of that dreadful night. Deliberately dismissing fear, she tried to organize her explanation as logically as the neat streets and decorated houses along the route. Stepping upon the porch, she touched the wreath with her gloved fingers before knocking on the door. Expecting her, Rod opened the door quickly, but stood staring at her as if seeing her for the first time. He looked handsome in his gray turtleneck sweater and black pants. A new haircut revealed the absence of the hearing aid. She knew from what Carla told her that he grew frustrated with the hearing device because the doctors had told him his problem was nerve deafness and said there was only a thirty-three percent chance of restoring hearing, and the aid was useless under those circumstances.

He finally offered with a gesture of his arm, "Come inside."

She slowly slipped inside the doorway, letting him help her with her coat and scarf. As he hung them in the closet, she rearranged loose tendrils of hair falling from the clip at the back of her neck.

"Where are the children?" She tried to keep her voice calm.

"Taylor is in his room on the computer, and Milly is in the basement playing with her dollhouse; but for now I'd rather talk with you without interruption."

"Of course." In spite of herself, her voice sounded weak.

They walked into the living room, and he offered her a seat in an armchair. He moved to the fireplace and stood with his back to her, looking into the fire.

"You said Joey came here to see you this morning." She found her voice and projected it evenly. She couldn't wait any longer. The suspense was almost unbearable.

He turned around, his eyes seeking hers. She lowered her lashes and started to turn away but instead lifted her head and looked up into his eyes, searching his thoughts.

"Yes, Joey came into the house...at an inconvenient time. He acted strange and asked odd questions."

She didn't say anything. Only her expression encouraged him to continue.

As the scene unfolded, she saw Joey, dressed in a black leather jacket and black pants, entering the back door when Taylor and Milly were leaving to walk Stewart. Not seeing Rod in the kitchen, dining room or living room, he called his name up the stairs. Rod, wrapped in his white bathrobe, came out of his bedroom where he had showered in his private bath.

"Joey?"

The two men faced each other for a couple of seconds, the older astounded at the other one's impertinence and a little embarrassed; the younger, with something on his mind, was oblivious to his old friend's predicament.

"I'd ask you to sit down, Joey, but I'm kind of busy at the moment."

"That's okay. I just need you to answer some questions."

"Fire away."

"What's your relationship to Kailynn?"

"Relationship?"

"Do you consider her your employee, friend or girlfriend?"

This was the last thing Rod expected Joey to ask outright. "I think a lot of her..." he attempted to answer. "As both employee and friend."

"Do you have plans to be more to her?"

Rod, feeling heat rising in his chest, took a deep breath to control anger. "I have more respect for her than that."

"How's that?"

"Kailynn seems a bit younger and has never been married. She wouldn't regard a man battered by life with two half-grown children..." And as if thinking aloud he stated, "It wouldn't be fair."

"I don't want to see her hurt. I warned Agnes of that fact."

"Warned?"

"I told her Kailynn is a lady and delicate. I don't want anyone to hurt her. Understand?"

"You don't have to worry about me. I respect Kailynn too much to do anything to harm her."

"Good." Joey finally became aware of the older man's discomfort. "Sorry to intrude. Just had to get things off my chest and out in the open. Go back to what you were doing. See ya later."

Rod raised his eyebrows. "Okay, Joey. Take it easy."

"Will do." And he was gone as quickly as he had come.

Kailynn sat motionless in the chair near the fireplace, yet thoughts swirled through her mind, and inexplicable feelings surged in her heart.

"Do you know why Joey would come here like that asking questions about you?" Rod inquired, more than curiosity crossing his face.

"N... no."

"Are you dating him?"

"We went to church with the children and attended the Christmas program with everyone else. Other than work, the only place we've been is here with our families." She was actually thinking aloud more than she was answering his question.

"Why would he think we might be more than friends?" Rod continued questions of his own.

Her heart plummeted to her feet. She looked up at the painting of Emma hanging above the fireplace. "No reason...I can think of."

He paced back and forth for a few minutes. "I wouldn't dream...dream...of asking you to be more than a friend."

This was too much denial for her to comfortably sit through. She rose and moved slowly toward the doorway, and then half turned. "Are you certain of this?"

Rod, strangely enough, took her seat in the armchair. Looking straight ahead, he declared as if it were a vow, "I'm positive."

"Great," she stated as a mysterious directive to start dating Joey.

"Kailynn!" Milly's voice rang out. "I didn't know you were here! Are you staying for lunch?"

"No. I brought these letters to your dad, and almost forgot to give them to him." She pulled a couple of envelopes from her pocket, and handed them to Milly. "I have to hurry back to the store before I get fired! I'll see you later, Milly." She yanked her coat and scarf from the closet and swung them out the door.

Putting her arms through the coat sleeves while she walked, reality set in. *I know I'm not the woman Emma was, not even the woman Agnes is. Why should I entertain the hope Rod would think of me as a romantic partner? He has more important things on his mind like two lonely children and a struggling business. Besides, I didn't tell him about the accident. He probably wouldn't be a friend at all. Well, that's fine because the police didn't consider me at fault, not really involved. I'm tired of torturing myself with doubt. I need to put that night out of my head and Rod out of my heart! Obviously, Joey cares about me. A girl would be crazy to ignore that kind of affection. Lord, please help me to someday know Your plan for me, and help me to want Your will."*

CHAPTER SEVEN

Kailynn continued to enjoy her work, purposely tuning out unsettling thoughts; and pleased Joey when she agreed to dinner and watching the fireworks with him on New Year's Eve. She chose a long creamy beige dress sprinkled with small blue flowers and a matching light-weight coat, the only adornments were small gold earrings and her cross. Her hair was swept up with a butterfly clip, but she let tendrils loose at the temples and the nape of her neck. A perfume reminding her of violets permeated her clothes. She smiled in appreciation when she saw Joey wearing an attractive dark blue suit complementing his dark hair with its hint of blue luster.

They dined at a new South Charleston Christian supper club called The Anchor. After prayer, they ate their salad and steaks in silence listening to the lovely contemporary gospel music. When the rotund owner, Henry Burgson, recognized Joey he asked him to sing. At first the singer declined, declaring Kailynn might feel neglected.

She assured him, "No, Joey. I would love to hear you sing unless you'd rather not tonight."

"I'm always looking for an excuse to sing! Isn't that vain of me?!"

She smiled. "On the contrary. It's very commendable that you're always ready to share your faith in song."

Mr. Burgson had quite a few CDs; and Joey selected one instead of the piano. It was a sweet song about the loving presence of Christ. Kailynn was almost certain she was where and with whom she belonged. What could be more perfect?

On the bank of the Kanawha River rimmed with spectators, Charleston streetlights along with holiday lights outlined the bridge; and boats added sparkle to the night. A local orchestra played current romantic music while the people waited for the countdown and the fireworks to begin. When she looked upriver toward an especially beautiful boat decorated in the state colors of blue and gold, her eyes caught sight of Rod in a silver jacket standing with his children among the excited people. For a moment, the stringed instruments and woodwinds echoed the secret chords always sounding deep in her being at the sight of this man. Unaware of time, she heard the music swell into Auld Lang Syne and fireworks exploding in the air. Joey bent his head to gently touch her lips in a quick, sweet kiss.

The first week school was in session neither Kailynn nor Rod mentioned the children. Morning devotions were short but helpful; and the prayers, especially for customers, sincere. They worked quietly together when necessary, but most of the time they worked separately, their minds on the task at hand or their customers. That is, until Friday when Taylor and Milly met Rod at the shop because Agnes had a dental appointment.

Taylor had gone into the office to see his father, but Milly eased beside Kailynn who was kneeling, carefully arranging ceramic gifts – angels, biblical figures and doves among the many – in a new glass case.

"Kailynn…" Milly's young voice was soft, as her full lips in a pout formed the name. Her eyes looked sad.

"Milly, are you feeling alright?"

"Yes…" The little girl seemed listless. "Why don't you want to stay with us after school? Don't you like us anymore?"

Kailynn closed the glass door, and hugged Milly to her. "Of course I like you," she reassured the little girl. "I love you. Your dad and I didn't discuss the situation any further."

Taylor's voice, steady with purpose, spoke behind them. "Well, why don't you discuss it now with all of us?"

She became aware Rod was standing beside Taylor, and that Agnes had entered the store. She felt at a disadvantage, still kneeling on the floor.

"The dentist is running behind and I have to wait at least half an hour." Agnes tried to change the subject.

Rod offered a hand to Kailynn, helping her to her feet. "We were discussing the possibility of Kailynn staying with the kids at our house after school."

Agnes smiled sarcastically. "I think she would have come to your aid by now if it were something she wanted to do, Rod."

"Excuse me," Kailynn interrupted. "Does this discussion include me? Then I think I should be addressed directly."

Rod and Agnes both looked stunned.

"For one thing, I was of the impression I was no longer needed on the home front. For another, that you, Agnes, had everything and everyone under control."

"Not everyone, Kailynn. Merely my household," Agnes responded pointedly.

Rod cleared his throat. "We didn't have a chance to finish the conversation concerning the children, and it goes without saying that we will all understand if you can't fit it into your schedule, Kailynn. Won't we, kids?"

"Yeah." The youngsters' tone indicated they were anything but understanding if their beloved sitter chose not to come to their house.

"But we would appreciate it if you could stay. I promise you will feel needed and wanted," Rod's voice teased threateningly.

"You bet," Taylor added.

"How can I refuse such a request?" Kailynn asked.

"Very simply and effectively. You don't have to do this." Rod stated. "The children will still be your friends and your job here is secure as long as you want...." He hesitated. "But I will pay you well if you accept the responsibility."

She smiled. "I really mean it. I can't refuse. There is nothing other than the work here I would rather do!"

"Yay!" Milly almost jumped around until she saw her father's warning glance.

"One thing," Kailynn requested. "Could we wait until Monday afternoon?"

"Sure," he agreed. "I planned to take them to our history museum today anyway."

Agnes smiled excitedly. "Oh that sounds marvelous, Rod! Do you mind if I reschedule my appointment, and accompany you? I know my dentist won't mind today, and it's only a check-up."

"Sounds like fun," Rod approved. "We could stop off for ice cream."

Kailynn suddenly felt forgotten and a little out of sorts at the merriment with which the four left the store together.

Rod phoned her on Saturday when she was off work and asked if she would like to go with the children and him to see Carla who was still in the hospital due to afterbirth complications. "I've cleared it with Joey already," he informed her.

She assumed he meant leaving the store in Joey's management. "Fine. I have a gift for the baby. I was waiting for him to come home."

"We were too, but they've had to keep Carla a little longer than expected. I talked to her this morning, and she's feeling better. She'll be coming home in a couple of days. But I thought we should visit her after all this time."

"True. What time would we leave?"

"I'll pick you up at one o'clock."

"Good. See you then."

~   ~   ~

The enjoyment of the ride together was evident. Rod appeared relaxed for a change and laughed easily. Kailynn sat back in the front passenger side of the car feeling comfortable in her soft leather coat and khaki slacks. She wondered if Agnes had experienced this sense of family yesterday. She sobered, glancing at Rod's handsome profile as he talked.

He noticed her abrupt change in mood. "Are you and Joey getting along?"

"I suppose."

"Don't worry about today. I asked Joey if it would be all right to bring you up here, and it was fine with him."

"Why did you ask Joey?"

"Since he practically interrogated me, I was afraid he would mind."

"Rod, he doesn't own me. We aren't even engaged."

"But you might as well be from what I saw New Year's Eve." They heard gasps from the back seat, and both wished they had steered clear of this subject.

"We're here, kids. Straighten up," Rod instructed.

They all entered the hospital noiselessly, Rod ushering them into the gift shop. He bought a beautiful arrangement of assorted flowers. They stood motionless in the elevator, and walked softly on the carpet toward the desk where a security guard sat.

When Rod informed the guard of their intention to visit, he was told that Milly would have to stay in the waiting area. Taylor did the unthinkable and noble thing for a new teen who desires to be included as an adult. He decided to stay behind with his sister. To Kailynn, this decision exhibited true growth toward maturity.

Expecting visitors, Carla had changed from her plain blue and white hospital gown to a fancy yellow gown and robe with many layers of lace. She smiled happily from her propped-up pillow. At first, Rod and Kailynn's attention was solely for Carla, but soon they were completely fascinated with the tiny blue bundle with its miniature toboggan pulled down above the eyes. Do you want to hold him?" Carla urged.

"If you open this package," Kailynn said. "Hope you can use another blanket and a sweater set." She carefully lifted the baby's head with one hand and his back with the other until she cradled the small wonder in her arms. "He's so fragile."

Carla held the blue sweater set up. "Aww…This will look pretty on him when I take him to church, and I'm sure I'll need every blanket I receive."

"That's good," Rod said. "Because that's what the kids chose."

"'Where are the kids?" Carla asked.

"Out in the waiting room. They were anxious to see you, but Milly wasn't allowed back here."

"Kailynn, carry the baby please. Rod, help me out of this bed and into those slippers. Let's go to the nursery. I'll have the nurse take him, and ask if the children can come see him through the window."

"But Carla, should you be walking? You could just buzz someone," Kailynn suggested.

"Honey, I have to at least walk the hall!" Carla exclaimed. "I've been cooped up in this room and on this bed too long! Besides, I want to make sure the kids get to see the baby."

It took the four of them a slow stroll, but they finally were able to watch as Milly and Taylor, still in their jackets, stared in awe at the newborn as the nurse lowered her arms on the other side of the glass.

Back in the hospital room, Carla was once again sitting up in her bed, and asked Rod if the business continued to grow. He told her about Joey's changes and Sara's employment.

"How did things go at home during the seminar?"

"Great. You know Kailynn was there. The kids had a wonderful Christmas because of her."

Again, people were talking as if Kailynn weren't in the room, but she kept her peace.

"Did you have a good holiday, too, Kailynn?"

"I had the best time of my life. Milly and Taylor are really special kids."

"They are. And I guess you and Rod hit it off pretty well and became good friends."

Rod and Kailynn looked uneasily across the bed at each other. He spoke first, "Pretty good."

Kailynn nodded in agreement.

Carla's eyes widened as she looked from Rod's flushed face to her friend's blushing cheeks, and then back again to Rod.

"We'd better get back and see what mischief Joey is up to." Rod put a stop to unspoken questions.

Kailynn leaned over and kissed Carla on the forehead. "If there's anything we can do for you, let us know. You're always in our prayers."

"Thank you." Carla's eyes misted over. "You all are very important to me and always will be."

Rod patted her hand. "Same here."

They talked about the baby on the drive home, and Rod revealed that he missed Carla at the store. "It's ironic. You wouldn't have come into our lives if Carla hadn't left the shop."

"That's not necessarily true. You hired Sara, didn't you? Eventually, your business would have picked up. Hopefully, you'd found the wisdom to hire me."

They grinned at each other, and the backseat audience giggled.

It felt good and comfortable to be with this family again, but a foreboding tugged at the back of Kailynn's mind.

CHAPTER EIGHT

The first day back at the Websters, Kailynn had left work early in order to be there to prepare a snack of apple wedges, cheese and caramel dip for the children. She had fifteen minutes for herself, and went into the living room for devotions. Milly had left Emma's book lying out on the bookcase for her; and she sat down in the armchair with it alongside her Bible. "And we know that all things work together for good to them that love God, to them who are the called according to his purpose." Romans 8:28.

Emma had written, "We see through a glass darkly as the Bible says, and it is difficult to know all the answers and reasons for unhappy times, but Romans 8:28 is our assurance that all things work together for good when we love God, and I do love God. So much so that I can hardly keep my feet on the ground. I'm thankful my family and I have this promise to hold onto."

Kailynn knew, too, that she loved God with as much of her heart as possible for a human, and held fast to this promise for herself and those she loved.

Taylor said the word "cool" when he entered the house and found her there offering him a snack, and Milly bubbled over with the day's school news.

When Taylor started off with Stewart, Kailynn suggested, "When you return, let's get the homework done and out of the way. Then, the rest of the evening is free. OK?"

The children were so relieved to be home for the afternoon and evening, they readily agreed.

After homework, Taylor wanted to spend time in Googling something on the computer for an upcoming paper. Kailynn checked to make sure he was scanning the encyclopedia.

Once in her own room, Milly took a book from her book bag to show her sitter. Immediately the young woman's face wreathed in smiles and her eyes softened as she shared a memory. "Anne of Green Gables. I remember the pleasure I had when Mother read this with me once." The book was attractively bound in green and adorned with flowering, intertwining vines. She read the first paragraph.

"Read more, Kailynn, please."

They curled up on the bed cushions and Kailynn began reading for both of them. This was the way Rod found them a couple of hours later. He heard her voice reading as he topped the stairs and moved quietly to Milly's door. It was intriguing in tone, and causing pictures to form in the imagination as she grew deeper into the story. As he edged closer to the doorway to see them cuddled together her voice registered surprise.

"Oh no, Rod. Should I have cooked a supper? I lost track of time."

"I left the store a little early, and picked up hamburgers and fries for us all. It won't hurt the kids to have fast food this one day. They can eat a healthy meal tomorrow. Not that you have to cook it for them."

"I really don't mind as long as I eat with them, too. I've developed an amazing appetite in this past year, and those hamburgers smell wonderful."

"Well, I can't imagine lettuce and tomato and onion being harmful. If you put it in a bowl it's called a salad." Rod justified his choice.

"I think the meat, especially a regular habit of ingesting the meat, is what people find objectionable, that and the grease, of course. But, oh, what a delicious form of protein!" She helped him feel better about his treat for them.

By then, Taylor was bounding down the stairs with them, anticipating the meal.

Milly piped up, "Daddy, did you buy orange drinks too?"

"Only one, Pumpkin. For you. We have cola already."

"Goody!" She almost flew into the kitchen.

While they ate, Rod turned curious eyes on Milly. "Why were you bothering Kailynn with reading to you? You've always been a good reader."

"But, Daddy, I wanted to hear Kailynn read it out loud. It's better than television or radio!"

"Hmm... I have to give you that one, pumpkin." Directing his attention to Kailynn, he asked, "Have you ever thought of reading publicly, Kailynn?"

"No! I've read books all my life. It's an activity I've used to compensate for missing out on other things."

"I think it's more than compensation. It's a talent."

"Thank you, but I've never considered myself talented."

"Well, it's time you change that opinion of yourself." Rod looked out the window as if in thought, and finally said, "I have an idea, but let me run it by Joey before I say anything."

"Should I be offended again?" Kailynn asked, with a half smile.

"No... It has to do with the store."

She didn't feel offended, but she dared to joke. 1"Just do me one favor."

"Yes?"

"Don't tell Agnes about the hamburgers and fries!"

He gave her a wry smile, and the kids laughed knowingly.

~ ~ ~

The next couple of mornings at the store were more relaxed. Everyone smiled easily, and the work was pleasurable to Kailynn. On Wednesday afternoon, she had brownies in the oven for the children's snack, and was mixing up a meatloaf for supper. While the meat baked, she helped Milly with a couple of math problems. Then the little girl asked Kailynn about devotions.

"Why are devotions important?"

As Kailynn explained their importance to her own day, Milly thought of two more questions, and then three more questions. Kailynn found herself telling the story of Christ and what He meant to her own life. Pure joy flooded her soul as she related her salvation experience and the peace Jesus gives her day by day in the midst of trouble or gladness.

When the telephone rang, her voice answered on a happy note.

Rod chuckled. "I caught you at a good time. Could I ask a favor of you?"

"You may ask." She pictured him sitting at his desk, grinning at her playfulness.

"I've received a shipment late in the day, so I'll be running behind. Would you go to the church with the kids tonight? I'll meet all of you there, and eat supper after prayer meeting is over."

"I'd love to, Rod."

"Is there a negative ending to that sentence or are you actually agreeing to go?"

"No. I would really love to go to that church with the children."

"My request isn't inconvenient?"

"No, Rod."

"Oh, oh. Your tone is changing. I'd better get off the phone before you change your mind, too!"

It was her turn to breathe a soft laugh. She smiled to herself as she placed the phone on its charger, envisioning him busily checking invoices and hurriedly removing items from boxes with family and church on his mind. She was glad she had worn her denim skirt and blouse today. Many of the women wore lovely pant suits there, but not in her parents' church. However, she sensed that to gather together to worship, pray and support each other was the priority.

She hadn't thought she would sit alone in the service. Milly and Taylor went immediately to their respective youth classes. The congregation sang *I Love To Tell The Story*, and she meant every word. As testimonies and prayer requests took over the meeting, Rod slipped into the seat beside her. A couple of women in the pew in front exchanged glances. Kailynn wondered at their mysterious facial expressions, but when it came time to greet one another with handshakes, they joined others around Kailynn and Rod sincerely welcoming her there. After

Bible study, prayer requests and prayer, the whole congregation sang again. This time, the hymn was *Bringing In The Sheaves*. Besides the wondrous trip down the aisle by a young man with short cropped hair, blue jeans and tee-shirt seeking salvation, Kailynn noticed people going forward making a public confession of faith and rededicating their lives to Christ. Why did she still feel a need to tell Rod about the night of the accident? Was it God prompting her to tell him, or was this her selfish desire to unload on a man who probably needed to put that night behind him and move on with strength to raise his children and run his business? Looking at Rod's noble profile again, she prayed, *Oh God, you know I love you and I love this family. I don't want to do anything to hurt them. Help me to understand Your will...* Suddenly, Taylor and Milly joined them, and they all walked home.

It was a clear, cold night. Holiday lights had disappeared, but the constellations sparkled brightly in the sky. When they passed Agnes' house, Kailynn asked where the talented lady had been tonight.

"Oh, she is rarely there on Wednesday nights," Rod informed her, then added, "She couldn't shine on Wednesdays."

Kailynn didn't know what he meant exactly, but she didn't pursue this line of conversation lest he have the impression she is a gossip. She tried to change the subject. "Where was Joey?"

Rod slowed his gait and stiffened his shoulders. "I should think you would know."

"No. Why should I?"

He ignored the last question, answering only her first one instead. "He is singing at another church revival this week. He does that kind of thing often."

"Daddy used to sing at revivals, too," Milly spoke proudly.

"I think you need to go straight to bed since you have school tomorrow morning, Milly," Rod instructed, as Kailynn realized they had neared the porch steps.

"I'd better head for home, Rod. Meatloaf, mashed potatoes, and green beans are in the refrigerator for you." Kailynn said goodnight to the children.

"Wait up," Rod commanded. "Get in the car, Kailynn. Taylor, lock up and watch Milly until I get back."

Not knowing what to make of Rod's brisk manner, she didn't say anything as she moved toward the car.

They were silent as they drove through the streets toward the interstate. Once on their way to St. Albans, the quietness was deafening to her; and Rod shot a glance in her direction, catching her eyelids lowered while she was wishing the radio was turned on to a station. He, feeling as awkward as she, finally turned on the radio, and music filled their little upholstered enclosure. Voices sang smoothly of love and hearts yearning for love. At first, they were both uncomfortable, but as the words and string instruments blended into a memorable song, they stole looks at one another. Rod pulled the car into the Richardson's drive. Their eyes searched questioningly the face of the other, and held to the end of the song.

Rod came around to open the passenger door, and walked her to the porch. He put a hand on her shoulder whispering, "I'll see you tomorrow at work."

She discovered she still possessed a breath to say, "See you."

The next day, Rod and Joey revealed their plans to their clerks to start a weekly Story Time. The idea included Kailynn reading the latest Christian preschool book and Sara would have a corresponding puppet show. A discussion ensued whether or not they should also have a simple craft with the same current theme for children to take home to remember their experience. Joey said that for the most part he would run the store. Surprising everyone but Joey, Rod said he would lend a hand to ensure the success of the Story Time.

Kailynn had never seen this side of Rod; and was amazed at the enthusiasm as well as the creativity he exhibited when discussing crafts. He offered to help with puppets when necessary, suggesting background music.

Kailynn put Joey off when he asked her to dinner Saturday evening, saying she wanted to examine some of the preschool books for the first program, and work up a puppet play with Sara and possible craft with Rod. She was willing to offer one hundred percent of herself to this program. No one could talk her out of volunteering herp weekend without pay.

Sara was also excited, anxious to design various puppets and stage settings with Rod's artistic help.

~ ~ ~

The next two weeks brought children and their mothers, grandmothers or sitters into their new activity room where the staff had cleaned out storage boxes and supplies. Chairs for participating adult employees set against a wall under a poster displaying the latest bestselling preschool book. Chairs lined the opposite wall also for each adult accompanying the little ones. Bright curtains adorned the top of the small windows; and new, brighter light strips lit up the area cheerfully. The tots sat on colorful mats in a semi-circle on green carpet while

Kailynn read. She then led them to sit in the same fashion in front of the puppet stage normally hidden behind folding doors. After she introduced the play, the puppets mimed to background music. Giggles rippled throughout the store. On these days, Milly was able to join the group because it was scheduled in the late afternoon, and assisted in any way she could.

The staff soon noticed a significant increase in sales: books, bookmarks, CDs, trinkets such as gold crosses, mustard seed necklaces and key-rings, praying hands and all gift items besides many books for adults as well as children. Carla and Taylor volunteered to assist Joey with customers. Everything went well until Sara strained her lower back lifting a couple of boxes too heavy for her small frame. It was clear that Rod was alarmed and controlled a rising temper. They all knew he had warned the women to fill the boxes only to a level and weight safe to handle, both for the employees and the customers. After a visit to a chiropractor, Sara resumed light duties excluding boxing and lifting heavy objects. For this reason she traded places with Kailynn, asking her not only to read to the children, but to work two puppets while Rod worked the other two. She said she would introduce the play.

Not realizing she would kneel behind the puppet stage, Kailynn wore her green and gold dress. She always tried to make the day special for the children. She sat back on her heels waiting for Sara to finish her conversation with the little children. Rod switched on the music, and signaled with his index finger up to his lips for Kailynn to move slowly when they approached the stage with the puppets. They listened intently as Sara began the introduction. Facing each other, Kailynn's blue-green eyes stared into his dark blue ones; and she became aware that he was closing his lids. Pressing his lips tightly together, he seemed to be listening for the cue. He opened his eyes, abruptly indicating with the frog puppet for her to draw back the stage curtains for him to begin the show. It was fun, but she was glad when Sara's back was strong again.

The staff didn't mind the occasional slow day in the store since they were now busy the rest of the week. These seemingly long days happened when the area experienced bad weather such as storms and heavy rain. It was on such a day while Kailynn browsed through the books that her whole body, clad in a blue smock and long denim skirt, practically tingled with the thought of how much her life had changed. That is, until she remembered the way her circumstances had turned around and the events which had led to her transformation flooded her memory, drowning out the joy. She nervously checked her low pony-tail, pulling it down on her neck and tightening the clasp. Opening a devotional with trembling hands, she moved toward the plate-glass window, looking out at the downpour. Rain pelted the glass and streamed down the pane reminding her of teardrops. She knew she needed to find the right time and place to tell Rod everything. A solemn expression shadowing her features in the overcast light, she clutched the book to her heart. In that moment she felt eyes gazing in her direction. Slightly turning, she saw Rod sitting in a relaxed position on a high stool, dressed in a denim shirt and blue jeans, with a large tablet propped upon his knees. He sat sketching; and the subject was her!

All morose thoughts fled from her mind as she recalled Carla whispering to her, when Kailynn had inquired about his artwork, that he hadn't sketched or painted portraits since his wife died. Excitement coursed through her body, heart, and mind. She couldn't wait to tell her new friend about this breakthrough!

CHAPTER NINE

Agnes stood at her double windows in her front room, but the pouring rain, driven by the wind, kept hitting harder by the minute and distorting any view she may have seen. She always felt isolated when it rained. If there had to be precipitation at all, she preferred snow as long as the temperatures remained in the thirties, and she could look out her windows at the trees, houses and the warmly clad people passing by, or go out to clear her porch. Now, however, she felt punched in the stomach. She turned toward the decorative mirror on the wall, and stared at her reflection, just to see a human being standing in her living room. There she was, a tall red-haired figure in her floral print housecoat. *No need to change clothes, now,* she thought. *No one is going to come to the house in this weather. People seldom do stop by even in good weather. That's why my church is so important to me.*

It's a chance to socialize with people. She peered closely at the hard, obviously unhappy and unsmiling image. Her freckles were showing. They were light but they were nonetheless still visible without her make-up. Her husband had said they were cute, but she was always convinced he was too enamored with her singing voice to ever notice her flaws or find any fault in her. She felt she had fooled him for years. Noticing the small lines at the corner of her mouth, she once again remembered that when she smiled they were diminished. She smiled now to prove it to herself, careful not to crinkle the fine lines around her eyes.

Dropping the smile, she walked over to her mantel and picked up her husband's picture. She gazed at the distinguished man with gray hair, wearing a blue suit. Strange, a person really couldn't tell that she had paid quite a bit of money for that suit. It was just dark blue, making his eyes look a darker brown than in real life. "This is all I have left of you, my dear," she spoke aloud. "It's all I have left of you, and it's a pose with a fake smile. Where is the grin as your face lit up when I would enter a room? All of your pictures are frozen in time, the fleeting expressions gone for good. I am left with handsome frames which have no life in them. I thank God for memories, but once a memory runs like a reel through my mind, there is nothing of you in reality." She grimaced. "I can bear this loss of you, sweetheart, except when it rains. When skies darken with clouds and rumble with thunder, a knot forms in my stomach the size of a fist, and my throat tightens, but no sobs heave forth. No tears fall with the rain, dear. I steeled myself far too long for you."

Putting the picture down in resignation, she walked back to the window. The hard drops of rain against the pane and the sides of the house were the only sound she could hear. She remembered that it had rained the day the doctor told them he had only three months to live. It was very much like a popular TV show, only the physician handed him papers instead of a rose, and in reversal, might have added, "Say your goodbyes now."

Nothing in her whole life or what she had always referred to as her marvelous marriage, had prepared her for this parting with her life partner…this finality. For all the great songs of faith she had so proudly sung, she had at that time questioned if she would ever see him again in eternity. Suddenly her thoughts went a different direction. *This is the reason I understood Rod's emotional sense of loss on losing Emma. No one else could understand it better than me. Certainly no twerp of a girl who obviously hadn't experienced any of life's sorrows.* Coming out of her melancholy as the sound of rain softened and the rivulets slowed, she straightened her posture, narrowed her eyes and tightened her lips. *I must and will protect that family from little, prissy women with infantile infatuations.*

As a beam of sunlight broke through the clouds and shone through her elegant living room, sending a sparkling aura over the delicate glassware, she turned on the radio, letting music flow through the house. *I really need to dust,* she thought. *Should keep busy. Maybe tomorrow will be better. You never know what difference a day might make.*

CHAPTER TEN

A long conference table for crafts, which Rod gave much thought, dominated the center of the activity room in the book shop. Through the week they would all spend some time cutting out shapes or preparing supplies. Sometimes Kailynn, herself, would have a craft idea to enhance the story. They tried to keep to a basic theme. It was just such an idea that brought her to the Webster's doorstep on a clear crisp Saturday morning.

Seeing the front door open a little, she used the knocker instead of ringing the doorbell. No one responded, but the knocking caused the door to swing open even wider. Hearing a voice raised, she thought someone may be telling her to enter. Stepping into the living room, she followed the direction of the voice coming from above the stairs, stopping short outside Rod's room. He was not talking, but singing! His voice was throaty and husky on certain lower notes, and strained on the higher. The result was a heartbreaking, soul-stirring sound. She recognized the song *I Must Tell Jesus*. He sang of telling Jesus all of his trials, that he couldn't bear his burdens alone. She knew instinctively she no longer could ever hear the hymn without also hearing his plaintive cry recorded in her mind. If he only knew how touching his heartfelt singing voice had become! Yet she knew he would be mortified if he knew she or anyone had heard. She felt like a sneaking intruder, retreating as noiselessly as possible. The song stopped when the front door creaked, and he called, "Taylor, are you back already?"

She barely made it past a neighbor's elm tree before she turned to see Taylor and Milly walking Stewart at the foot of the knoll, near Agnes' property on the other side of the Webster house.

Sensing Joey would not be put off any longer without Kailynn hurting his feelings, she suggested a pizza place that particular Saturday night. She, in a black turtleneck jersey and black skirt and he, in a plaid shirt and blue jeans, sat in a booth across from each other. They sipped colas while waiting for their pizza. Temptation almost overcame her to ask if he knew Rod could sing. True, it was a different range, but nevertheless poignant and actually on key. He held his notes even if it wasn't as long as he might have in the past. She remembered him ending lines by letting his voice change from the last note with a slight break to a lower or higher one. Afraid she would blurt out this new revelation, she pushed all thought of the Websters or the business to the back of her mind.

The conversation turned to the end-time prophecies. Joey had a book with him, and turned to several pages, and produced a small new testament from his shirt pocket. She had the feeling that he had planned to discuss these events with her. It was a stimulating conversation in which he was willing to listen to her bits of knowledge, current information and opinions. She certainly liked this quality in him. He was a good listener as well as a good witness.

After a while they selected upbeat music on the old-fashioned jukebox; and ate their pizza laden with extra cheese, pepperoni, mushrooms, black olives and green peppers, commenting from time to time on the tasty sauce. The date was over early and with a kiss on her cheek, he was gone.

She stood on the little porch looking at the moon, wondering if Rod ever took time to view the glowing orb's reflected light outlining the dark clouds drifting across the sky. Did he ever think of her? She shook her hair loose, letting it fall to her shoulders and surround her face as though to shake loose her thoughts. She slowly walked inside the house, closing the front door quietly behind her. She was ready for sleep, ready for dreams.

~　~　~

Kailynn opened her eyes, but slowly stretched every muscle in her small frame, and lay there peacefully in her bed until she remembered her plans to go to the petting zoo with Rod and the children. Sitting upright, she reached for the clock on the bedside table. She hadn't set the alarm last night. Jumping up and grabbing clothes out of her drawers, she headed for the shower. A streak of excitement zigzagged through her body. *I have a life now,* she reminded herself. Trills of laughter bubbled out of her as she stepped into the bathroom.

They all wore jeans and tee-shirts with hoodies to the farm topping a hill on the outskirts of St. Albans where a family ran a small petting zoo for parents to bring their children for hands-on experience with animals. Milly squealed at the sight of the gentle black and white pony, and enjoyed feeding it a carrot after a short ride. Taylor screwed up his face when the bearded man informed them that when the goat ate roughage, he would regurgitate and then chew whatever he threw up.

"Eew!" Taylor acted like his stomach was going to toss up its contents.

As they leaned over the split-rail fence, watching black Vietnamese pigs, one came over with a small grunt for Kailynn to pet him. After a while, he actually maneuvered a wooden stool over toward the fence and waited, obviously wanting her to come inside.

The man laughed. "That's the smart one. You really can go inside if you want, and pet him." Then he added a warning, "I wouldn't ever jump into a pen with grown hogs though. They're capable of rooting you so much you could get hurt, or worse. These little fellers here at the farm are safe enough for you."

She climbed over the fence and stepped onto the stool. As soon as she had landed on the other side, the pig rubbed up against her affectionately. She ran her hand over his back. When it was time to move on to other animals, she didn't want to leave. Rod smiled fondly at her when she referred to the pig as her baby. She would have liked nothing better than to take him home with her. During part of the tour they dodged chickens to stop at the barn for the children to hold and pet the small animals such as rabbits, guinea pigs and hamsters, happily giving them treats.

When they dropped Kailynn off at her house, she said, "I seem to always owe you thanks, Rod."

"And I you, Kailynn. A big thanks." He smiled contentedly. "I'd better get these farm hands home so they can clean up before bedtime. Hope you have as good an evening as the day you've given us.

"Likewise, Rod. See you later." She smiled as she exited the car.

A sore throat threatened Kailynn's participation in the preschool program, turning into the common cold. She used cough drops with zinc, took Garlic tablets and drank chicken soup, finally ending up in bed on a Saturday. Disheveled in the long warm robe to ward off chills from a fever, she answered her mother's summons to the overstuffed living room. There stood Rod still in his jacket, grinning at her attempt to hide her tissue in a pocket.

"When I drove past Agnes' driveway, I saw Joey and stopped to say hello. He told me you were spending the day in bed with this cold." He handed her a thermos. "I brewed this special herbal tea to return the favor when I came home from the seminar. I found the recipe in Emma's little box on the counter. Hope you like the taste."

"That's the one I used, but you didn't get a chance to drink it."

"I saw it the next morning and was thankful that someone could be so thoughtful. It really is very effective in easing symptoms; and helps a person rest." He had been talking in hopes of relieving her tenseness.

"Thank you. Won't you sit down?" she asked, in her hoarse voice.

"No, thank you. As I told your mother, I have to get back to the kids. Hope you feel better tomorrow; and we see you Monday."

"Thank you, Rod...." Bringing out a tissue, she suppressed a sneeze.

He nodded and backed out the door.

After he was gone, she glared at her mother before she waddled toward her room as if it were a refuge from the world. A quizzical expression crossed the older woman's face, but neither spoke.

She started to the nightstand with the thermos when she saw her reflection in the mirror. No make-up, not even natural color – just an ivory white complexion – dark hair with damp curls clinging around her face and neck, puffy eyes and swollen pink nose. Setting the thermos down on the table, she threw herself backwards onto the rumpled bed. After about half an hour, she made herself drink the hot, soothing liquid. Rolling over on one side, she switched her disgruntled thoughts off and fell into a much needed sleep.

~   ~   ~

On a Tuesday afternoon Taylor's principal called his father at the store. His English teacher wanted to explain his final grade with someone right away. Rod had just received a shipment and needed to check the invoice. Seeing his predicament, Kailynn stepped forward. "Rod, this is perhaps presumptuous of me, and the teacher may be reluctant to talk with me; but, if you want, I'll go to the classroom as his sitter and one who is responsible for Taylor doing homework."

"I'd appreciate that, Kailynn. You and I can discuss the grades this evening. I'll call the school; and tell them to expect you."

Taking her smock off, she put on her navy blue jacket and straightened her hair in its clip, glad she had dressed up a little this spring day.

Having reported to the office, she now sat in a chair beside the teacher's desk. He was a young dark-haired, dark-eyed man, a mid-year replacement in this class.

Taylor sat alone in the rear of the classroom, in his usual seat near a wide window. Milly waited at the door.

"I would rather talk to Mr. Webster...but Taylor's grades need explanation..." The teacher hesitated.

"I understand, Mr. Corbin, but Mr. Webster is unavoidably detained; and since you insisted this matter warranted immediate attention, I'm here. I'm Kailynn Richardson, Taylor's after-school sitter and responsible for his homework hours."

Mr. Corbin placed a row of test papers on the desk for her to examine.

"I'm puzzled, Mr. Corbin. These are excellent scores!"

"Exactly. But Taylor's final grade will drop a whole grade level."

"Why is that?!"

"He daydreams. When I'm up at the board teaching, he doesn't pay attention. He gazes out the window at the trees and the sky, and loses interest in the subject."

"I still don't understand." Kailynn was appalled that this boy would be punished for wounding a teacher's ego when his grades were glorious. "If Taylor isn't paying attention to you, how would he learn enough to score one hundred percent on your tests?"

The teacher looked from the papers to Taylor who sat staring gravely down at his own desk.

"That's a strong point," Mr. Corbin asserted.

She turned around in her seat addressing the boy. "Taylor, would you wait with Milly in the hall for a minute?"

Without a word, Taylor rose and walked, carrying his notebook and text in his right hand close to his leg. It struck her that he had grown a couple of inches since she first saw him in the ICU waiting room.

She turned again toward Mr. Corbin. "If Taylor appears distracted at times it may be because he lost his mother in a terrible car wreck last winter. The change of seasons and holidays, no doubt, cause memories to surface and probably create a keen longing to share time with her again. Even if this is so, he obviously pays sufficient attention to learn during your class. As a matter of fact, you must be doing a great teaching job to be able to penetrate his pain long enough for him to learn as much as these papers indicate."

Mr. Corbin's facial features expressed sorrow; and his tone was apologetic. "I'm sorry he has suffered such a horrible loss. You're probably right in your assessment of his attention level. Between the two of us, maybe I can make the misunderstanding up to him some way." He rose, extending his hand in dismissal. She knew he felt like thinking about this new information alone.

"Thank you." She shook his hand firmly.

CHAPTER ELEVEN

The children were out of school on Friday due to a teacher's meeting; and Kailynn had the day off from the store so she could spend the entire day with them. An apron covering her lavender sweater and gray tailored pants, she baked apple cinnamon muffins in the morning for breakfast; then, started frying chicken, cooking green beans and boiling potatoes to mash before mixing with the boiled eggs for mustard potato salad. Rod had asked her to prepare this meal, saying he would be home for lunch. She felt secretly glad he wanted to eat with them, but she thought all this food was an extremely heavy meal for a lunch. She popped the biscuits in the oven close to ten minutes to twelve. While they baked, she sliced tomatoes, wondering if Rod liked anything else with fried chicken.

Since Milly and Taylor, both in sweaters and jeans, spent the morning in the basement moving things around, she imagined they were cleaning out the storage area. Ascending the steps into the kitchen, they looked at the clock and winked at each other.

"That fried chicken smells really good, Kailynn, but could I have a peanut butter sandwich?" Taylor grinned.

"What? Taylor, you can't mean that! The biscuits are done. We'll eat this meal as soon as your Dad arrives!" she exclaimed. Standing with hands on her hips, she blew stray strands of hair out of her face.

"Yeah, we know, Kailynn," Milly spoke, "but it might be awhile before we eat; and I'd like a sandwich, too!"

"Milly!" Kailynn stared, mystified, and starting to feel frustrated. "Did your Dad call to say he would be late?"

Taylor pulled the curtain back, looking out at the street running past Agnes' house. "No. He won't be late. He's right on time and here."

Kailynn, stupefied by their request, froze in place in front of the stove.

Rod entered the house through the kitchen door. He, too, wore a sweater and jeans. "Wow. Everything smells good enough to eat now, but we better wait at least a couple of hours. How about sandwiches?"

Kailynn felt as if it were really time to wake up from this ridiculous dream.

"Taylor, is the picnic basket cleaned and ready to pack?" Rod inquired.

"Yes, Sir!"

"Milly, do you have the large plastic dishes ready?"

"Yes, Sir!" Her voice piped up excitedly.

"I picked up the drinks and ice on my way home to put in the cooler."

Kailynn's eyes widened; and her mouth dropped open. Surely they wouldn't take off on a Spring picnic with the food that she had spent all morning cooking for them all to enjoy!

Rod noticed she was staring at him, her eyebrows raised in question. "Please don't say you won't go with us, Kailynn.

"But don't you have to go back to the store?"

"No. Joey and Sara are there. I figure this is a good day to spend time with the kids."

"Where are you going to picnic?"

"Gauley."

"Gauley River?"

"Actually, Carnifex Ferry Battlefield. There's a wooded trail we like to follow. The view of the river is awesome."

"Please come," Milly pleaded. "You were going to stay with us all day anyway."

"I'm not sure I'm dressed appropriately."

Rod assured her. "You're dressed fine. In fact, downright lovely."

Milly giggled and Taylor rolled his eyes before a smile crept into them.

Kailynn protested. "Something tells me lovely won't endure hiking a trail.

Rod handed a plastic bag to her. "That's the reason I bought these jeans for you...with Carla's help, of course."

"Even Carla is in on this conspiracy! I'm outnumbered!"

They all laughed, and began packing food.

Agnes watched from her front porch as they merrily loaded the car with all the picnic supplies and play equipment. The children sat in the backseat with tail-wagging Stewart who appeared to laugh, too, with his mouth open and his tongue lapping out at their smiling faces. Kailynn rode up front with Rod. They all waved at their neighbor as they passed, but she stood unsmiling, gripping the broom as though it were a weapon. A chill rippled across Kailynn's carefree spirit. As the interstate highway took them to the wondrous wilds of West Virginia, where nature was busy painting the hills and valleys with the pastel shades of Spring, she relaxed, dismissing any dark or foreboding thoughts.

Kailynn had only seen Gauley River from car windows. Her family had attended church picnics and reunions beside man-made lakes, but never hiked or enjoyed swift rivers for obvious reasons. They had babied their daughter much as she resisted. Perhaps they were sure this was the way she'd lived long enough to safely reach the day of her surgery. However, she suddenly longed to see the river close up, but Rod parked at the far end of the picnic area and steered them to restrooms and a shelter quite a distance from the expected view. The sight of the yellow forsythia bushes along roads, wild flowers waving in the breeze, and mountain pines in the mist beckoned the poet in her. Blossoming trees and vines heightened her senses and hinted at even more fascinating summer foliage. She alternated between wanting to run through meadows, something she had often daydreamed of doing when a child, and standing with arms lifted up to God, the Creator, in worship and thankfulness. Joy filled her heart to the brim and overflowing onto the features of her face. She suddenly sensed Rod and the children staring at her with expressions of delight.

When they were seated around a picnic table under the shelter, Rod led the blessing over the food, thanking the Lord for Kailynn who had prepared it. She couldn't help but open her eyes at that inclusion and to watch him continue the prayer. By the time they finally ate, their appetite was sharpened by time, fresh air and the smell of long awaited food. The chicken was well done and tender. The green beans were flavored with a touch of chicken broth the way Rod requested. The mustard potato-salad was thickened but creamy, and the biscuits were fluffy with melted butter. Though Rod and the children drank lemon-lime and cola drinks, she chose to drink the iced tea she had made earlier in the day.

When they had finished eating and re-packed everything, they all agreed it was time to walk the trail and burn up calories. At home, they would have felt like taking an afternoon nap, but nature sparked their energy to exercise while enjoying plants, rocks and streams. Milly kept picking flowers; and Taylor found stones he declared were fossils or arrowheads or unique formations. Stewart's ever-sniffing nose never left the trail.

"Hey, Kids!" Rod cautioned with a grin, "Leave something for other tourists!"

Kailynn followed the trail in a world of wonder all her own. Blue jays screamed their aggressive nest-building plans! Once in a while she caught a glimpse of cardinals, the brilliant red male and his female with a hint of red blush complementing her mate's vivid colors. She reached out gratefully for Rod's strong yet gentle outstretched hand, guiding her to animal tracks or a particular tree he wanted her to examine. His artistically long fingers traced a leaf and explored tree bark as he talked in low tones, practically mesmerizing her. She had never experienced such an awe-inspiring hike in the woods; and sometimes felt like she must be dreaming, though if she were, she didn't want to wake up.

They came out of the woods near a restored, gray construction housing a Civil War museum. Taylor was disappointed when they soon discovered it was closed, but Rod promised a Fall visit during a re-enactment. Kailynn didn't share her distaste for re-enactment of what must have been a bloody war, brother against brother, heartache for mothers, sisters, wives and sweethearts - brave women, praying, sewing and gathering supplies for their men. But this was an important period of their country's history and therefore a fascination to many Americans, so she said nothing, lest she spoil the day for Taylor. She had to admit to herself, though, to a curiosity concerning the objects on exhibit.

They strolled back along a paved road leading from the museum to the picnic area. Milly and Taylor ran to the overlook, yelling at one another about the whitecaps, and pointing to where the river wound in the distance. As Rod and Kailynn approached, the kids ran off in search of swings and trees to climb. The steep mountains surrounded them. The river spread out below, flowing swiftly around boulders jutting out of the water. It was obvious she was enraptured with this scene. A soft Spring breeze ruffling her hair, she turned to see a look of enchantment mirrored in Rod's face. He smiled his own appreciation for the beauty around them, and slipped his arms around her in a light embrace. She closed her eyes as his lips lightly pressed against her forehead and then brushed past her temple. She never wanted this moment to end, opening her eyes again when she felt him pull back slightly.

"We'd better leave," he whispered.

She nodded.

The four of them loaded the car again, this time quieter, but content. They were almost ready to roll when a tiny meow from a nearby bush lured Milly away.

"Milly!" Rod warned. "What have I told you about investigating noises in the woods?"

"But Daddy," Milly whined. "It might be something stuck or hurt."

Stewart's whole body danced around as he barked and sniffed the bushes.

Rod pushed aside the brush and brought forth a small long-haired black and white kitten. Her green eyes were big with fear. "Why do people drop these little, helpless animals in the woods?"

"I guess they think they can run free and somehow find food," Kailynn ventured.

Taylor added, "Agnes says the shelter puts kittens to sleep as soon as they come in because there are too many."

Milly began to cry. "Oh, Daddy, let me take her home. Please!"

"Milly, you're overly tired. It was a mistake to stay too long here." He examined the kitten as best he could. "I don't think she's been here very long. We'll examine her thoroughly before we let Lady near her."

"Lady doesn't like other cats," Taylor reminded them.

"Well, she will have to like this one," Milly said petulantly.

"There are some things you can do to help her mother a kitten," Kailynn advised. "But it's too late to discuss them now. I'll try to help you tomorrow."

Everyone agreed. Taylor controlled Stewart in the backseat with Milly holding the kitten beside him. Kailynn and Rod listened to the radio as the vehicle traveled the miles through the twilight soon deepening into darkness. When they pulled up at her house, she asked him to stay with the children as she saw herself inside the house.

"Okay, but remember you promised the kids you would help with the kitten tomorrow," Rod reminded her.

"I won't forget. Goodnight, Rod. I truly had the time of my life today. Thank you."

"We all had a good time, thanks to you." He smiled. "Goodnight."

CHAPTER TWELVE

"Would you like a cup of coffee, R.L.?"

"Don't mind if I do." R.L. realized he felt comfortable in Agnes' living room. She was always hospitable, and seemed to like having a man around the house.

When she had poured the hot liquid for them, she looked toward the windows. "Why don't we take our coffee out on the porch? It's such a lovely evening, not too cool or too warm."

"A splendid idea, Agnes."

When they settled in the deep padded wicker chairs, R.L. took a sip of coffee. Looking at her, he said nonchalantly, "Tell me about your husband."

She looked down at the skirt of her blue flowered dress for a moment. Raising her head, she exclaimed, "Oh no, you don't, R.L! You first. Tell me about your wife and how she died, and then *maybe* I'll tell you something about my husband!"

He grinned. "Okay, I'll go first, and then you have to tell me about your husband. Fair enough?"

"Fair enough." She smiled.

Holding his cup on one denim covered knee, he leaned back further in his chair. "Martha was a hard-working wife. Oh, I don't mean she worked outside the home or anything, but she was a coal miner's wife, and did everything from cooking, mopping, sewing and washing clothes. She was faithful to do everything she could to make our life better. Why, she even painted walls alongside me and scrubbed our wooden porches herself when-"

"Did she never relax?" Agnes interrupted.

"Oh sure, sure. I guess I make it sound like work was all she did. There were plenty of times we enjoyed watching the sunset or the moon rising over the mountains together. We went to church every time the doors opened."

"Did you have any children?"

"A son. A fine son I took fishing every chance I got."

"Where is he now?"

"Nevada. I never visited there, but he came home a few times." Quietly he added, "I've never gotten used to him being gone away from home." Pausing again, he stated as an afterthought, "He's got a life of his own now. I guess I don't figure in it very much."

"Surely he came home when his mother died."

He nodded. "Yeah, but it hurt like crazy when I had to watch him drive away."

"How did Martha die?"

"It was sudden-like. Here, laughing one day and gone the next. I couldn't believe it. Felt kinda guilty too. I knew she was having chest pains once in a while, but she would take aspirin and everything would be fine. Back to normal, you know?"

They sat in silence for a while, watching the silhouette of birds flying through the crimson glow of sunset.

"Okay, enough about me. Now it's your turn," he said.

Agnes rolled her blue eyes sheepishly in his direction, obviously not wanting to talk about her husband or her experiences during his death. "Well, I don't know which is worse, a sudden loss or a lingering death. I didn't want to let go of my husband until he wasted away and appeared to suffer more every day. I began to regret all the years I had worked in an office instead of staying home. But that was silly. He worked in an office in the same building, and our hours were alike."

"Yeah, it seems we go through a period of guilt over one thing or another during that time. You said it took a long time for him to pass. I bet that was a stressful situation. Did you cry a lot?"

"No. I felt the stress alright, but I wouldn't allow myself to cry. I was afraid to cry." She squared her shoulders, and sat up straighter in her chair. An icy expression glazed her eyes as she looked at him. "I was determined to keep my resolve to stay strong for him. As time passed and it neared the end, I didn't want to show any signs of weakness. I didn't want him to worry about me. Later, I had to stay strong and clear-headed to get through the funeral and financial arrangements."

"How did you sleep?"

"Sleeping pills, until I caught myself automatically doing things in the house, but not remembering when I'd done them. Also, I was scared he would need me and I would be in a deep sleep or make a stupid mistake because of the pills." She looked out again as the moon rose over the hills. "When I was finally alone, I felt that if I gave way to emotion I might fall apart."

He glanced at her profile before his eyes followed her view of the moon. "Yeah, I had to stay strong, too. But I'm not ashamed to admit I cried. I cried when I'd walk into the kitchen and see her apron where she hung it last. I cried when I saw the material she didn't have time to finish still lying on the sewing machine. I remembered how excited she was the day she purchased the right shade of rose-pink for a dress pattern she had picked out at the store. Most of all I cried into her pillow when I went to our bedroom alone that first night."

"But you seem so strong, R.L."

"Do I? I guess I cried it out and then accepted the reality of my loss. Every time memories flooded my mind, instead of letting myself drown in them, I thanked God right out loud for the years Martha and I spent together." He sat upright in his chair. "Oh, I still feel the pangs of grief once in a while. Of course, I do. But I pretty much fell into another routine. My routine, not the one Martha and I had lived. Things got easier for me when I stopped expecting to see her in every room or on the porch waiting for me to come home."

Agnes stood up and placed a hand on his shoulder. He met her sad smile with one of his own. "How about a slice of apple pie with your second cup of coffee, R.L.?"

"Sounds good to me. But one more question."

"What's that?"

"Where are you from? I mean, originally?"

"From what you would call a coal camp." She said in a wry tone of voice. "My Papa died of Black Lung and my Mama's heart gave out when I was eighteen. I ended up working in a local store while I went to a community college in the next town." She shrugged her shoulders. "I focused on typing classes, and raised my baby brother."

"You did a good job."

"Well, maybe, but having a good voice and singing in the church really lightened my load. As soon as I graduated, I landed a secretarial job in Charleston. I met my future husband in that office, and moved Joey and myself into an apartment in this city. Life for me really began at that point."

R.L. reached a hand up to cover hers. "How 'bout that pie now, Agnes?"

She smiled down at him and nodded.

In the kitchen they sat across from each other at the table with coffee cups and plates of pie in front of them, both enjoying the warmth of new companionship.

"Rod was really fortunate you happened to be out on that awful road that night, R.L. You didn't need to follow up and keep track of the family's welfare after the accident. Most people wouldn't. They would simply drive away and go about their business."

"I'm not made that way, Ms Agnes, and I guess neither is Kailynn."

"Kailynn?"

"Yeah, you know. She could have forgotten about that terrible road and the weather conditions. She sure would want to forget the close call she had that night with her car sliding sideways and all. But apparently, she wanted to check on the family, too."

Agnes' eyes widened and her pupil's grew larger with every word. "Oh…yes… I guess so. But it took her long enough!"

"That's understandable. She probably didn't know the family's name or address. But one thing for sure, when she did know, she made a beeline straight to them."

Her eyes narrowed at this statement. "She certainly did."

As Agnes approached the brick apartment building on Kanawha Avenue near the river in Charleston, she mentally rehearsed what she would tell Joey. Pressing the button for the elevator to take her to the third floor she reasoned, *Surely he will see Kailynn for the conniving liar she has been all along. I hate to hurt him, but it's better neither he nor Rod have anything to do with that woman any longer.* Walking through the corridor, she searched for efficiency apartment 322 in anticipation of his shocked reaction and justified anger toward that deceptive woman.

"Sis!" Joey opened the door wide inviting his sister into his one room apartment.

Her eyes swept quickly over the bed dominating the room, the kitchenette off to the side, the dresser with a small television, an arm chair and a corner lamp stand that ran from the floor to the ceiling. "Oh, Joey. Surely you're not comfortable here. You know you could have plenty of room at my house. This place doesn't even have a view of the river."

"Now, Sis, we've been through this before. It's a perfect base for my comings and goings. Besides, you couldn't stand my returning home at 2:00 am off a road trip. You would be on pins and needles waiting for me, and then wake up every time you heard me open the door. It's not like I'm never at your house every week. We have dinner together all the time. So stop bellyaching, sit down and tell me what is so important it brought you to my building and to my door this time of the night."

"Sit? Where?"

He grinned. "You sit in the arm chair, and I'll sit on the bed."

"Oh, fine then! Where do I start?"

"From the beginning?"

"No. I'll start with R.L.'s last visit to my house."

Joey moved the shirt he'd taken off and sat down on the bed. He was glad he was still wearing his tee- shirt and gray slacks.

"Well," she began, "R.L. and I were chatting over apple pie at my kitchen table when he let it slip that Kailynn was on the same road the night of the accident that took Emma's life. Her car slid on the ice, Joey, probably forcing Rod's car off the road over the embankment and onto the tracks below. R.L. talked like I already knew she was present that awful night and called it a close call for her."

Joey moved closer to the edge of the bed and was bent over listening intently. His blue eyes were blazing in the lamplight.

"I didn't let R.L. know I knew absolutely nothing about Kailynn's presence that night." She paused, looking into his flaming eyes. "And I doubt Rod is aware she was there. He would have said something before now."

When Joey didn't say anything, she added, "Don't you see, Joey, Kailynn is a liar!"

"No, Agnes. This discovery of yours does not make her a liar. She probably has her reasons for not revealing the truth right now."

"I'll say!" Agnes was suddenly on her feet with her hands on her hips. "She's a gold-digger, no doubt!"

"A gold-digger? Oh *come on*, Sis! What gold? Rod has a nice house, but he's trying to make ends meet the same as the rest of us."

"Well, he does have that lovely home and his business."

"Agnes, *think* a minute. Kailynn is an only child and will inherit her parent's property which is paid in full. She doesn't *need* Rod's house with its mortgage."

"Well, nevertheless, she didn't tell the *truth*, Joey. You can't deny *that*! She is deceiving Rod. When I think of those poor children…"

"Now, Sis, you are not to meddle in this business. You hear? If anything, you should pray for all of them."

She pursed her lips and looked away from him.

"Do you hear, Sis?"

"Yes, I hear, but I don't approve of silence in this matter."

"Approve or not, I want your word that you won't say anything about this to Rod or anyone. It explains a lot of Kailynn's behavior and decisions, and I want her to have a chance to cope with this situation on her own terms."

"Oh, all right, Joey, but I don't know how long I can stand by and watch that family struggle in her web of deception."

"Actually, Rod and the kids appear to be climbing out of a very dark place and finally finding light at the end of an extremely long tunnel." Joey rose and offered a hand to his sister. "Go home, Sis, and get some rest. Maybe in the morning you will see things in a different perspective."

"I doubt it, but I'll go and try to sleep on it. Maybe *you* will see things differently too, my little brother!"

They hugged at the door; and after her descent in the elevator, Agnes left the building a little more subdued than when she arrived.

CHAPTER THIRTEEN

S tretching leisurely in her bed Saturday morning, Kailynn suddenly remembered her promise; and hoped the Websters had slept late, too. The bathroom mirror scolded her by its unkempt image of wearing makeup to bed; and she scrubbed her face thoroughly with a washcloth. Satisfied when the towel left a shining complexion, she donned blue-jeans and a short-sleeved yellow sweater.

Her mother entered her room as she swept the sides of her hair up with a clip. "Are you going somewhere, Sweetheart?"

"To the Webster's house. I'll probably grab something to eat there."

Her mother, smoothing the apron protecting one of her many flowered dresses, followed her into the bathroom and watched while Kailynn brushed her teeth and applied lemon lip balm. Waiting until her daughter sat on the bed putting on white socks and white walking shoes, she dared to ask worriedly, "Aren't you spending a lot of time with them, Honey?"

"Don't you like them, Mother?"

"Of course I do. Just you're gone so much and-"

"I'm home every night, Mother."

"I know you are, but when have you spent a whole day with your dad and me? Not to mention that nice young man who called last night."

"Joey?"

"Yes."

"Hey, I see that nice young man every day of the week; and I do go out with him on an occasional Saturday. I spend most Sundays with you and Dad, though." Kailynn looked at her mother suspiciously. "Is there something else bothering you about the time I spend at the Websters?"

Her mother grew uncomfortable. "I just don't want you to get hurt, Kailynn."

"Did someone else call you, Mother?" Her tone demanded an answer.

"Well, yes. Agnes Naylor. She didn't want me to tell you. But I didn't promise I wouldn't."

Kailynn sighed. "What did she say?"

"Only that she was worried you might grow attached to the family. She said you shouldn't be investing so much time and emotion into a family that needs someone more experienced than yourself."

"And that would be Agnes, right?"

"That's the impression I got, Baby."

"Mother, I like it when you call me Baby, but I'm not a baby. I'm a grown woman."

Her mother looked abashed. "I'm sorry."

"Don't be sorry. I'm merely making a statement of fact. I've grown up." Kailynn hesitated, but decided to continue. "I am fond of that family. I love them. If that breaks my heart, I'll keep loving them and praying for them. You can't shield me from hurt." She felt compassion at the stricken look on her mother's face. Her tone softened as she added, "That's part of life. Don't you see, Mother, I'm living life now. Its ups and downs."

"And Joey?" her mother asked anxiously.

"He's my friend, and I'll continue to see him if he wants. But I'm in no hurry for anything permanent."

"Love is pretty compelling, Kailynn," her mother warned. "Remember that nothing is more powerful or enduring than God's love. I would feel better if we prayed together before you leave the house."

Nodding in agreement, Kailynn took hold of her mother's hands.

When she stepped off the bus Kailynn sensed the sweet Spring breeze against her face. Feeling lighthearted, she went into a pet shop for kitten shampoo, a bottle of worming treatment and a plastic syringe. Then, she stopped by a florist shop for pink and yellow tulips to plant. While there, she noticed butterfly windchimes on display in the window. Milly's delighted expression on seeing anything with butterflies flashed into her mind. Smiling broadly, she purchased one.

Milly flung the front door open as she was setting the flowers on the porch. "Kailynn! You came to help us with the kitten!!" The little girl wrapped her hand around hers and led her to the kitchen where Rod stood at the stove frying sausage.

He looked pleasantly surprised to see her. "I set a place for you, but I didn't know if you would show or not since we were so late getting home last night."

She smiled; glad to see him in jeans and sweatshirt, ready to do yard work. "I bought tulips for the flowerbeds.

They're pink with a touch of yellow that should complement the Easter lilies along the fence."

He pulled out a chair for her to sit, and scooped sausage and scrambled eggs onto her plate. "Milly, run and fetch Taylor. Save the kitten until after breakfast. We'll take care of her before we work outside."

They chatted mostly about the kitten's antics, Lady's obvious disdain for this new family member, and Stewart's thwarted attempts at acquaintance. Kailynn helped Rod load the dishwasher before they all filed down to the basement where Milly's kitten was curled up on a pile of old drapes. Kailynn gently picked up the little wide-eyed pet. A low, growling hiss, hardly audible, warned the intruder. Yet ,the animal was docile and submitted to a warm bath and towel drying at the laundry sink. Lady, leaping up on a small table to observe the young animal in the bath, enlarged her eyes, put her ears back and scampered quickly up the stairs. Kailynn administered the worming medicine as everyone gathered around watching her drop the liquid successfully into the tiny mouth and stroke the tiny throat until the kitten swallowed.

"When you want Lady to like her," Kailynn advised, "bathe both cats, then leave them alone for a couple of hours. Lady will groom herself, and then her natural maternal instinct will probably cause her to begin grooming the baby. Eventually, she will want to teach her other things, too."

"You sound like you've had a lot of cats." Rod was fascinated with her almost professional manner.

Embarrassed, she stated, "You don't own cats. If you respect their feelings and show them you care, they honor you with their presence and affection." She faced them, still blushing. "I wasn't allowed cats. Mother thought they would steal my breath away. I poured over pictures instead and read many books about animals."

Changing the subject, she asked Milly, "Have you named her yet?"

Milly's eyes misted over. "I've decided to name her Kailie after you."

Placing the newly named kitten in Milly's arms, Kailynn carefully hugged both. The kitten emitted a meek meow. "Don't forget to take her to the vet for her shots."

"Oh, I won't forget. I promise!" Milly bent her head over the kitten, running her index finger along the kitten's white nose and the white patch just above, stroking the damp, dark fur between the black ears. Kailie reciprocated with rubbing the side of her head against the little girl's hand.

Taylor gave his sister a brotherly pat on her back and his dad a wink.

With the kitten settled on a cushion in Lady's old basket with newspaper not far away, they headed outdoors. The first thing Kailynn did was balance herself on a lawn chair to hang the windchimes on the porch. A vocal sound behind her nearly made her fall. Rod stood there, red faced.

"Who put you up to this?!" His tone demanded an answer with as much force as he could muster. He tore the windchimes down and held them in front of her face.

"What do you mean? I just wanted to surprise Milly."

Milly ran onto the porch and put up a hand to silence her father. "Daddy, I showed Kailynn all my stuff and pictures of butterflies. She doesn't know about Mommy's windchimes!"

Understanding flickered over Rod's features, but his cheeks remained red, now from embarrassment. "I'm sorry, Kailynn. You have no idea the significance windchimes hold for this family. I am sorry for my tone of voice and behavior. Can you forgive me?"

"Of course," she responded, yet still felt confused.

He handed the windchimes to Milly. "Hang these in your room, Milly. Okay?"

"Sure, Daddy."

When her father had gone back to the yard, Milly turned to Kailynn with an apologetic look. "You had no way of knowing, Kailynn, but Mommy loved windchimes and hung them all around the porch with her hanging baskets. When she left us for heaven, Daddy couldn't stand to hear them. He took them all down and put them in a box in the attic."

"Oh, I'm sorry, Honey. No, I didn't know. I would never want to upset or hurt your family."

"I know." Milly gave her a hug.

While clearing the flowerbed of debris, Kailynn was conscious of finches making a nest under the eave on the porch. An orange-breasted Robin hopped around looking for the birdbath. The scent of lilacs already filled the porch and front lawn area with their delicate perfume.

Pushing the lawn mower to where he wanted to start near the sidewalk, Rod tossed a clean pair of work gloves into her lap.

She smiled up at him. Trying them on she found them a little large for her small hands, but she would use them until she began planting the flowers.

Spotting a flowering plant in a shady area near a corner of the house, she asked, "What is the name of that plant?"

"You haven't ever seen a Bleeding Heart?"

"What?" Kailynn looked perplexed.

"A Bleeding Heart plant." He summoned her with an index finger to come closer to the flowers. "See, its blossoms are in the shape of hearts which hang from the stem. Often they are red, but I planted pink ones for Milly. She likes pink hearts all over everything."

Kailynn examined the plant in so much awe that Rod began to grin in amusement. He realized that he wanted to share many such moments with her for a long time to come. Life was full of wonder for this woman. He wanted to feel that wonder again.

After Milly had brought Kailynn a small hand-rake, and a trowel, she and Taylor picked up trash and dug up dandelion roots though the girl spent more time adding to a bouquet of the yellow flowers, calling them "sunshine in the grass".

The soil was warm today and Kailynn felt the satisfaction planting often gives a person. Seeing the tulips in their rows, brightening the property with their pink and yellow colors joy of accomplishment lifted her already soaring spirit.

Using the weed-eater along the edge of the front walk, Rod noticed the cheerful flowers and Kailynn's delight. "Taylor," he directed, "go get the sprinkler can full of water for Kailynn."

"Aye aye, Sir!"

When Taylor returned, however, he had planned mischief. Striding over to his sister who was kneeling in the middle of the yard searching for more weeds, he announced, "We gotta water this daffy-dill!" With this announcement, he turned the can upside down and dumped the water over the blond head.

Drenched, Milly sputtered; and after collecting her wits, went off like a high-pitched siren, "Daddeee!"

Rod hadn't seen Taylor mischievous for so long he stood dumbfounded by this prank.

"Daddy!!"

"Okay, Pumpkin. Taylor, you wasted that water. Go get Kailynn more. This time for her flowers."

"Yes, Sir." Taylor grinned.

Kailynn jumped up. "Hold on, Milly. I'll bring a towel."

While Milly dried off and Kailynn watered her plants, a Blazer pulled in front of the house. A male voice called up the walk, "The Easter Bunny is here!" R.L. carried a large basket with big chocolate eggs he had purchased from his church.

They were surprised when the eggs were not only decorated with pastel flowers, but also with each of their names. Kailynn's face transformed from guarded reserve to amazement when she saw her name written across an egg decorated with small pink roses.

The corners of R.L.'s eyes crinkled. "I was hoping you would be here today."

Roderick's eyebrows arched in silent inquiry.

"Kailynn was here when I stopped by before Christmas," R.L. explained.

"Oh," she changed the subject, "we'd better take these eggs inside before they dissolve in this unseasonable heat."

Watching the activity from her next door porch steps where she had been cleaning banisters, Agnes narrowed her eyes and set her lips in a straight line of determination. She marched up the walk, unnoticed by the chattering little group, but as R.L. turned toward the clicking sound of her sandals, her demeanor changed to carefully controlled tolerance. "Do you have one of those for me, R.L.?"

"Sure do! In the car, though. You are my next stop."

Agnes looked pleasantly surprised and pleased. "Thank you, R.L.! Do you think you could give it to me now?"

"Well, sure. Be back in a minute."

When he had gone a little down the walk, Agnes swirled toward Kailynn, no longer smiling. "Could I see you in the living room for a couple of minutes?"

Everyone's eyes were now on Agnes because her tone had taken on a hard edge.

"I suppose," Kailynn looked questioningly at Rod.

"It's alright with me, girls," Rod answered her unspoken question, but felt uneasy for some indefinable reason. "We can take R.L. into the kitchen for coffee and soft drinks.

Kailynn excused herself to wash her hands in the downstairs bathroom while Agnes paced back and forth in her khaki pants and plaid blouse under Emma's portrait. The younger woman composed herself before entering the room, asking the Lord to help her handle whatever was causing Agnes' agitation.

Instead of the couch or armchairs, Kailynn walked to a small polished reading table with two upholstered chairs. Sitting down in one of the chairs, she invited Agnes to sit across from her.

After looking at the younger woman's face, Agnes confessed, "Kailynn, I've been jealous of you." Tears sprang to her eyes and rolled down her cheeks, but she looked steadily into the unflinching blue-green eyes.

Kailynn sensed this was, however true, not a heartfelt confession, but a prelude to more; and she waited.

"I gave Joey my word, against my better judgment. He made me promise I wouldn't say anything to you or anyone about what R.L. told me. But that's silly. R.L. is part of all our lives. As long as you are around here there's a good chance he will mention it sometime, no matter what we do." She wiped her eyes and nose with tissue from her pants pocket. "It's like this, Kailynn. If you leave Roderick and the children alone, I won't ever reveal the fact you kept it secret that you were at the scene when they wrecked. You can keep your job, but you have to give up this cozy relationship you're building here. Understand?"

Numbness nearly dragged Kailynn's spirit down, and her heart sank for a moment. "I understand."

"Then you agree?"

Other words spoke quietly to Kailynn's mind; and she slowly rose and moved to the bookcase. She pulled out a card on which she had written scripture. "The Lord prepared my heart for this and even more. Perhaps it's out of context, but somehow it strengthens me for what I'm about to undergo."

Agnes cocked her head to one side, her eyes squinting as if she were shielding them from the glare of light, while Kailynn read the scripture. "Beloved, think it not strange concerning the fiery trial which is to try you, as though some strange thing happened unto you: But rejoice, inasmuch as ye are partakers of Christ's sufferings; that, when His glory shall be revealed, ye may be glad also with exceeding joy. I Peter 4:12, 13."

The purpose of this reading was completely incomprehensible to Agnes. "Well, Kailynn, what does this mean? Do you agree or what?"

"No. I will tell them everything myself; and take whatever condemnation I deserve."

Agnes jumped to her feet. "You would hurt them like that?! You're pretty selfish! You'd better rethink this, Girl. You would have no one, not even Joey."

"I will have God, Agnes; and they will have the truth and the comfort of the Lord Jesus."

"What is so serious in here?" Rod's voice interrupted their altercation.

"I'll tell you what!" Agnes offered vindictively. "I'm sorry, Rod, I didn't tell you sooner, but Joey made me promise not to say anything."

"What are you talking about, Agnes?" Rod demanded.

Kailynn tried to interject. "Rod, I want to tell you myself. If we could only talk alone, I-"

"She was there on the road the night you had the wreck. She may have even caused Emma's death!" Agnes accused.

R.L. crossed to Kailynn's side. "You didn't tell them who you are?"

"I wanted to..." she said feebly. She was near tears, but knew she had to be strong to endure. "The time never seemed right."

Taylor's face contorted in rage. "She was at the hospital, Dad, that night! In the waiting room. Milly and I saw her." Turning to her he bellowed, "You killed our Mom!!"

A different kind of pain than she had ever experienced pierced her heart.

R.L. put up his hand. "Stop right there. She did *not* cause the wreck, Rod. I was there. The authorities checked it out. Both cars slid at the same time. Kailynn could just as easily have gone over the bank too."

Rod nodded, still in shock by Agnes' unexpected response to his question, Taylor's outburst and sudden flashbacks of that horrifying night. Everyone mistook his stare for anger.

Milly cried out, "Stop it! Stop it! Agnes, you're a mean old witch!"

Finding her voice again, Kailynn spoke more calmly than she felt. "It's alright, Milly. Agnes wants what she thinks is best for you children. I should have told your father the first day I met him." She knelt as the little girl drew closer, allowing her to hold her arms with both hands as she looked into her eyes. "I've regretted being there that night. For a while I, too, believed I might have caused the wreck when my car slid toward them. But if I really had, it surely would have been an accident, and not deliberate. If I hadn't been there, I might not have known you, your Dad and Taylor and everything I've learned about living and loving from all three of you."

Standing, she looked at all of them. "I hope you all will someday forgive me for not telling you about that night sooner." She moved as though to leave.

R.L.'s voice restrained her. "She risked her life to try to save you and Emma that night, Rod. There wasn't anything anyone could do until help arrived except stay with you."

Milly cried out again. "No, Daddy, don't be mean to Kailynn! She couldn't hurt anyone or anything." Sobs tore her words apart and tears streamed down her face. She pulled at his shirt with both hands. "Please, Daddy. Don't be mad. Kailynn had a hard time. She had a heart operation... She had to have her heart fixed!"

Everyone's eyes flew wide open. Rod turned his stare to Kailynn's face. Her expression told him and everyone there that this was true.

Abruptly, Joey's voice boomed. "You broke your promise! Didn't you, Agnes? You broke your word!" When he had entered Agnes' house and she was gone and R.L.'s Blazer was in front of the Webster's dwelling, he had experienced a sinking sensation something like this might happen. "Well? Are you happy, now? Now that your gossiping tongue and jealousy has cut out the hearts of people I love?"

Agnes looked like she was hurting, too, but raised her red head defiantly. "Rod has a right to know; and she could have told him anytime. Isn't that right, Rod?"

"I think the kids and I need some time alone..." his voice weakened.

Kailynn's heart felt like it was crushed. She hardly knew when Joey slipped his arm around her shoulders, and escorted her through the room and out the door to his own car.

Deep, pitiful sobs wracked Rod's frame as he fell to his knees, grabbing the children close to him with both arms. There in a huddle the three of them cried, their sobs penetrating the windows and door, tearing the hearts of listeners.

R.L., who had patted Rod on the back without saying goodbye, now stood with his shoulders hunched near his truck. He told Agnes he would earnestly pray for them all.

Her chin began to quiver; and she nodded her head before his arms wrapped around her. In painful resignation, she leaned against his chest. "This isn't what I wanted. I don't know what I expected, but not this." She looked up at him in anguish. "Why do I feel so crushed, R.L.?"

"It's a hurtful situation. But God can sort out all the confusion. His peace surpasses all understanding. Give it all to Him, Agnes."

"Surrender all? Like the hymn we sing every Sunday." She raised her head and stood thinking about what that phrase really means. "Will you come pray with me, R.L.? I don't want to be alone in all this pain."

Holding her hand securely, he slowly led her home. Every now and then he would cover her hand with his other one, reminding her that God is great enough and His grace sufficient to straighten out each life involved. He reminded her, too, that Christ is a friend who stays closer than a brother, a better friend than himself, a friend who never forsakes. They went through her front door, ready to release their faith for answered prayer.

Joey drove Kailynn toward her home in St. Albans, but then crossed a bridge on the Kanawha, driving slowly full circle, and turning up the pavement winding around a mountain to a city park. He was in deep thought; and Kailynn's mind was momentarily suspended as she gazed out the car window. When he opened the door for her, she stepped out and onto a carpet of buttercups. She focused her vision into their tiny centers before raising her eyes to behold majestic oak trees, spreading their thick branches like a greater covering than the man-made shelters built throughout the park. Joey led her to a wooden bench. As they sat down, she realized it was built to gently glide back and forth. She watched the billowing white clouds drift across the blue sky. A soft breeze caressed her face. What could possibly be wrong on such a wondrous day?

They sat, moving back and forth for a while before Joey spoke. "You needed a quiet time to calm your fear."

She had thought he was going to say *nerves,* but she heard the word *fear* instead. Yes, she, even in her stillness, had felt fear. Fear of losing the family she had learned to love, their friendship, their emotional support. It was then she realized how much they were aiding her while she offered her assistance and her affection. She became aware of Joey's Bible open on his knees as he drew her attention to the third Proverb, verses five and six.

He read aloud, "Trust in the Lord with all thine heart, and lean not unto thine own understanding. In all thy ways acknowledge Him, and He shall direct thy paths."

"Trust Him, Kailynn." Joey's eyes sought hers. "Trust Him with your whole heart to heal this and any situation. Trust Him with your own life and what *He* wants to make of it, *is* making of it. Let Him guide and direct your next steps, each and every decision." He placed both his hands on her small shoulders. "He won't let you down, Kailynn."

She looked at him through tears blurring his visage.

"I thought I trusted Him, Joey. My life was busy in service. Everything I did I did for the Lord as the scriptures say. Every day I woke up to joy, grateful to be alive…no, no, grateful to really live life!"

"And don't you know the Lord understands that, Kailynn? He remembers that we are human and make mistakes. Yet, He sees the pure intent of our hearts."

Joey brought his hands down on either side of her arms. "Kailynn, when you live for the Lord no matter what your handicap might be, you are living the greatest life possible on this earth and the world to come. If all you can do is pray for souls or people's physical needs, prayer is the most powerful gift in the universe. Jesus, Himself, prayed."

Kailynn's spirit leaped up inside of her and bore witness to his words. *"Prayer and praise,"* she thought, *"Prayer and praise!"*

Joey saw her eyes light up with understanding and faith. He dropped his hands and touched the pages of his Bible. "Please forgive Agnes. She watched her husband's life ebb away, hiding her feelings every day from him. She steeled herself for him, and then for Rod and especially his children."

"I'd already forgiven her, Joey, thanks to the Lord."

"God isn't through with my sister yet. He's waiting for her to surrender herself and her talent to Him."

After a little while longer, they parted at Kailynn's home. She entered the front door, embracing her mother who, knowing her daughter's touch, understood. They knelt at the sofa to pray together.

CHAPTER FOURTEEN

The next few days passed slowly, as if time froze at intervals. At first Rod felt dazed, almost numb. He and the children stayed inside the house, doing only what was necessary, preparing plates of sandwiches with chips, yet only picking at the food. They made sure the dog and cats were fed, but the animals behaved as if they sensed that something had changed in the atmosphere, as the family members took turns letting them outside and opening the doors to allow them back into the house without their usual loving tones of voice, pats and strokes. Though the day was warm, Rod had absent mindedly slipped a thin white sweater over his head, and adjusted a pair of black slacks. Once in the kitchen, he began preparing coffee when he noticed the bag of chocolate raspberry coffee Kailynn had left behind; and, picturing her delight when she would take that first sip from a cup, he smiled for the first time in days. When he had poured his coffee into a mug, he walked into the living-room. The quietness filled the room. He realized that Taylor had started playing video games in his room again, though the boy's face showed no pleasure in the games, and Milly sat or lay on her bed leafing through books. Looking out the front windows he noticed the shower of blossoms wafting on the breeze, and remembered how he had looked forward to Spring. *Yes, I actually had looked forward to Spring again. Not long ago I didn't think it was possible for me to ever look forward to anything again.* He recalled the bare trees of winter. Ordinarily they and the overcast skies would have depressed him, but when he would come home after dark some days, he would see a lamp lit near the window, and feel, if not happy, a comforting peace that he was home and that Kailynn would be there. He then also remembered she had left the house with Joey. True, he had said the children and he wanted to be alone. He had known he would finally break down and cry. *But she left with Joey.* The thought taunted him. *Well, she probably should be with Joey. What business does a wreck of a widower with two children have clinging to the kind of joy Kailynn brings into the lives of others?* He looked around the room, and could envision her standing in front of the fireplace, looking into the flames or sitting in an armchair reading Emma's book, which now lay on the end-table where she had placed it. *Emma. What happened to the memory of Emma? I used to see Emma everywhere inside and outside the house.* He knew Emma would want him to live a normal, even productive life, and to encourage her children to do the same. In fact, it would hurt her if she knew that life had come to a stand-still for them all. He felt perspiration beads forming above his brow, and rubbed his forehead. He needed a break from the house, he and his children. It was then he made up his mind to spend Easter out of the state.

When Kailynn returned to work at the shop with some trepidation, Sara informed her that Rod had taken the children to Ohio for a visit with his sister-in-law, Nadine, on their Easter break. Since he hadn't called her, Kailynn assumed this news possibly and most probably meant he didn't want to see her. She also took this as her cue to hand a two-week notice to Joey who tried to talk her out of quitting her job.

"Kailynn, I'm sure you're misinterpreting their visit, and taking his oversight personally."

"Of course, I would take it personally, Joey. I was the babysitter; and he wouldn't call me about an Easter vacation? *Come On!* What other conclusion would I draw?"

"But you like your job, and you're good at it. Why give it up?"

"Joey, how long do you think I would like my job if I make Rod miserable by my presence?"

This line of reasoning finally silenced him. She smiled tenderly and patted his arm. "Don't worry. I will be fine. I'll have another job soon with you as an excellent reference. Right?"

He grinned and nodded, though his eyes remained serious.

She enjoyed helping customers in spite of personal difficulties, and she savored the time spent reading to children, thinking she might not have this pleasure much longer. She literally missed Rod's presence when she had to kneel behind the puppet stage.

Looking across the counter on Friday was Agnes, dressed in a stylish violet dress. She asked to speak to Kailynn whenever she took a break.

"I'm sorry, Agnes, but I plan only a short break to eat my lunch today." She felt dowdy in her khaki skirt and brown top, even if the t-shirt did display the scripture verse *Love One Another* in gold-colored letters.

"Please, Kailynn." Agnes appeared anxious. "I don't blame you if you refuse to give me the time of day, but I hope you'll give me a few minutes... I really need to talk with you."

Asking Kailynn to sit on a bench outside near the shop, Agnes began an apology. "I know you may believe this is pretense, but I really am sorry for my behavior and any unhappiness my words have caused you, Rod and the kids." Her features suddenly crumpled in tears. "I never meant to hurt those children. I've known Milly from the day of her birth. Now I just *have* to find a way to make it up to both of them."

"What do you want me to say, Agnes?"

"I want your forgiveness, and a chance to be your friend."

"I do forgive you, but as for friendship-"

"Kailynn, I have a new heart too, now." Her light eyes pleaded for understanding.

Kailynn arched her brows, questioning the meaning of this statement.

Agnes continued, "The book of Ezekiel 36:26 states it best for me. "A new heart also will I give you, and a new spirit will I put within you, and I will take away the stony heart, and I will give you a heart of flesh."

Kailynn was surprised by Agnes' change in reasoning and attitude, especially when her voice lowered humbly as she said, "And God has given me a new spirit, Kailynn. I want very much to be a good friend to you the rest of my life." She then did the unthinkable for Agnes Naylor. She leaned forward and hugged the younger woman. "Oh there I go again. Always about what *I* want. I'm sorry, Kailynn. It will take me some time to put God first, others second and myself last. But with His help, all things are possible." She attempted a slight smile.

Kailynn managed a little smile, too, as she patted Agnes' trembling hands.

Once she made up her mind to quit her job, changing her entire life, all the faith she had felt after Joey's conversation with her seemed to melt in the heat of such a final decision. *Surely this is a nightmare,* she kept thinking. *And soon I will wake up smiling in relief!* She wanted to stomp her feet and pinch her cheeks in an attempt to bring herself out of a frightful dream. *But no, it isn't a dream, and I have to live with the loss of a family who had come to mean the world to me...who had become my world.* Perspiration formed on her upper lip as though she had been running a futile race or lifting a heavy burden she couldn't quite carry. *Father, help me!* It was then she thought of Carla, and desired to speak with her above all other people as soon as possible.

Unsure how she had worked up the courage to contact Carla since deciding to leave the store, Kailynn sat in the corner of a back booth, facing the wall in the diner. How would she bring herself to tell her friend everything that has happened and the reasons for leaving her job? So far, she had only managed to text on the cell and ask for this meeting. If she had actually spoken to her on the phone, the knot in her throat would have betrayed her emotions. Her tremulous voice would have revealed volumes in only seconds.

When Carla entered, she stood uncertain in her black dress pants and one of the loose, flowered maternity tops she still wore. Not seeing her friend at any of the tables, she began searching the booths. When she stopped at the last one, Kailynn pulled on a blue cardigan over a gray t-shirt and folded her arms as if to comfort herself. Her jean clad knees squeezed together under the table. One look at Kailynn's pale face with its stark look of loss triggered an alarm in Carla's mind. She sat down across from this sad countenance. With an expression of real concern she ventured, "What's happened?"

For a full minute their eyes held. Perhaps, Kailynn secretly hoped for mental telepathy to spare her the trouble of having to tell and relive everything. Tentatively starting with that terrible night on the mountain road, she surprised herself when she suddenly began blurting it all out in a gushing torrent of emotion. Carla's eyes widened and narrowed at intervals as the truth poured forth and the stream of revelation slowed into pools of low, sad sobs. Their eyes stared across the booth as full understanding formed between the two friends.

"Would you like to order now?" The lilting tones of the waitress startled them both in its incongruity.

Blinking, Carla muttered, "Uh…coffee with cream."

Kailynn lowered her eye-lids. "Coffee…black."

"Anything else?" the girl asked cheerfully.

"Not right now." Carla dismissed the food.

Kailynn just shook her head.

"Okay! I'll bring your coffee in a sec." The girl swiveled on her toes and swung her sandy ponytail as she bounced away.

"Do you hate me for lying to everybody?" Kailynn's voice was self-incriminating.

"You didn't lie, Kailynn. You omitted information. That's all. There's a big difference."

"I don't think Rod sees it that way."

"Maybe not right now, but given time and space, he will. I know him."

"There is no time…and he will have all the space he needs. I'm done. I'm out." Tears sprang to Kailynn's eyes.

Carla stretched her hands across the table to cover her friend's. "Don't say that. You are too much a part of the family now, Kailynn. I hate to see Rod dropped into that sinkhole again and the children stranded again by separation."

Tears spilled from Kailynn's eyes just as the waitress set the cups of coffee in front of them.

"Will there be anything else?" The girl's voice carried a soft intonation, and her brown eyes were sympathetic.

Kailynn and Carla both shook their heads; and the waitress walked away. As each young woman held a cup between her hands, they sipped the warm liquid in silence.

~   ~   ~

"Whoa there, Woman!" Carla's husband cautioned. "You're pushing that soil down a little too firm. Those geraniums will have a hard time growing through that packed soil."

Carla raised her head from where she stooped at the flowerbed to look at Mike as though she were waking up from a disturbing dream. She had been mentally rewinding her conversation with Kailynn in the diner.

Mike started the baby's little swing swaying again. "Where've you been, Hon?"

She leaned back on her canvas heels, set the trowel down on the ground and took off her gardening gloves. Swiping dirt off her denim jeans and floral top, she exhaled a breath that sounded too much like a sigh.

"What is it, hon? What's on your mind?"

Noticing his summer navy-blue and white jogging clothes she wondered how long he had been back from his run and watching her. "Oh, nothing much."

"Now, Carla, I know you better than that. Come on, out with it."

"Oh, *okay*! Kailynn and Rod."

"What about Kailynn and Rod? Want to let me in on it?"

She looked away from him for a second. "I know we tell each other everything, but-"

"Yeah, and we don't want to stop now. Do we?" Mike's eyes gave her a dark warning look someone else may have misjudged as aggressive. The two of them knew it was a reminder of their agreement to be transparent with each other. Both had parents who were divorced because the couples kept secrets from each other, and soon drew apart emotionally and finally physically when they separated.

"I don't think Kailynn would want me to discuss the things she told me."

"You mean she asked you to keep them confidential."

"Well, no... not exactly. It was more of an understanding type thing between women."

"But if it's worrying you it's gonna worry me. And I don't even know what it's all about!"

When she responded with silence, he stated, "I *am* your husband, Carla. I'm not just anybody." His voice grew tender. "I'm your husband, honey."

She gazed into his tanned face earnest in its expression. Patting the ground with a hand, she motioned with her head for him to sit across from her. When he sat cross-legged in front of her, she recounted all that she knew about the predicament separating Kailynn from Rod and his family as well as the shop.

"So you mean, she's actually quitting her job and won't be at the bookstore any longer?"

Smoothing a blade of grass with her fingers, she nodded her head.

"Oh *man...*"

"That's not the worse part, Mike. Rod and the kids crashed again; and Kailynn, in spite of her faith, is wandering around looking like a lost puppy."

"She won't get another job like that."

"Exactly. Besides, I've been convinced since day one that God led her to our store and to the Webster family."

"Well, worry won't help that. Worry is a waste of time. What do you want to *do* about it?"

"*Do*? You can't fix *everything*, Mike. The truth is that if God brought them all together, *He* will keep them together."

"Without any help from you, right?"

Her brows furrowed.

"Sweetheart, don't you know by now that the Lord works through people ninety-nine percent of the time?"

"Don't you think that percentage is a bit exaggerated? Besides, Mike, I can't just barge right into the middle of their lives telling them to forget what's happened and move on!"

"No..." He puckered his lips. "But you can accept the role God is prodding you to play in the restoration of their relationship to one another."

"Is that what God is doing? Prodding me?"

"You're the one to figure that out. But worry is a waste of time."

"So, let's pray about them instead, and seek the Lord's will."

"You got it!"

Holding hands, they began to take turns praying, their golden rings glittering in the sunshine.

CHAPTER FIFTEEN

Easter rolled around; and Joey convinced Kailynn, Sara, and Carla along with her big brawny husband who carried Baby Michael, to attend the services at his church since he would be singing a solo. As they all entered the sanctuary, sun filtered through the multicolored glass, adding an aura to the spotlight over the pulpit. Purple cloth draped the large cross up front to remind the congregation of the supreme sacrificial lamb, and the ultimate victory as Christ came off the cross, out of the tomb and ascended to be crowned King.

Donated baskets of flowers ran along the aisles and across the carpet in front of the choir. Women wore dresses in their latest simple, classic style and soft colors adorned with small sprigs of flowers. Little girls proudly showed off their shiny pastel dresses. The men wore their nicest suits, many sporting new ties, and even many of the boys wore vests over white shirts, if not entire suits. The atmosphere was celebratory. Pastor Arthur led a heartfelt prayer of praise before they sang, *He Lives.*

The choir hailed everyone with *Praise Him! Praise Him!*

Joey stepped upon the platform, adjusting the microphone but leaving it in position. Kailynn had always noticed his broad gestures sang as much as his voice. He nodded to the pianist, and began singing in true triumph, *Christ Arose,* before singing the first verse. Everything about the service expressed exaltation, but the unexpected highlight of the service for Kailynn, was beholding Agnes Naylor rise to the occasion, pure joy radiating from her face. She stated in a clear voice that her song was a personal testimony of Christ's resurrecting power. Her voice rang out the melodious words of *He Keeps Me Singing.* She enunciated the words in the second verse meaningfully; and each time she sang the name *Jesus* in the chorus the name sounded sweeter. On reaching the last verse, she raised her hands to invite everyone to join her in the chorus.

Rev. Arthur delivered a bold message about the saving grace of a merciful Savior. He hardly looked at his outline as He spoke from a heart blessed with the prayer and praise he, too, had experienced this morning.

After the closing prayer, the people rose, shaking hands with each other. Kailynn and Sara were making over Carla's baby who gurgled and sputtered in contentment with so much attention, causing the women to laugh. In the midst of all this enjoyment, Kailynn's eyes wandered over the crowd dispersing, catching sight of Rod standing at the end of a pew toward the back of the left aisle near the windows. She hadn't expected to see him or the children today. He was looking directly at her, an expression of curiosity crossing his brow. The children were still in the pew, gathering their Bibles and program sheets. She decided to exit before they could spot her and spoil their lovely day. The line inched toward the vestibule, and she felt Rod's eyes on her back. Reaching the door, she shook Rev. Arthur's hand and smiled with genuine gratitude for a motivating message.

Catching up with her on the walk, Joey suggested they have dinner at the Anchor. Kailynn wondered how her parents would feel if she skipped an Easter meal with them and her relatives. She decided they would actually feel happy for her.

"Did anyone have any other plans?" she asked. "How about Agnes, Joey?"

"R.L. is spending the day with her. Didn't you see him sitting on the front row?"

"No, I didn't notice, but I'm glad they are such good friends."

The two cars pulled out of the parking lot, Carla and Mike following Joey, Sara and Kailynn. The day would almost end as perfectly as it began.

~ ~ ~

As Rod climbed the stairs in his house his heart felt heavy with the weight of worry over his children and the absence of Kailynn's friendship in their lives. Checking Milly's room first, he found her sitting on her window-seat where her dolls were once lined up for play. Now she sat looking out the window, herself like a forlorn little doll in her flowered pajamas.

"Milly." At the whispery sound of her father's voice, she turned her head.

"Would you come with me into Taylor's room? I want to talk with you both for a few minutes."

"She nodded her head, but didn't smile. "Sure, Daddy."

When he saw his son still in white t-shirt and jeans, Rod's heart hit rock bottom. Taylor was playing his computer game with an attitude of vengeance. Anger shot almost visibly from his physical posture toward his imaginary opponent.

"Hey, Tay."

"Hey, Dad." Taylor spoke without taking his eyes off the screen.

"Can you turn that game off long enough to talk with us?"

"I haven't won yet."

"Save it," Rod's voice rose in strength surprising even him.

"Yes, Sir."

Rod indicated with his hands for both of them to sit on the boy's bed. Pulling Taylor's computer chair over in front of them, he sat down. Looking at his folded hands, he kept quiet for a few minutes. He sent up a prayer to the heavenly Father, and asked for words to explain the situation to his children so they could stop losing ground they had, in his estimation, begun to regain.

"I know you both feel as if the roof collapsed on your world again." The dark looks he received affirmed this description immediately. "Yeah," he continued. "You feel disappointed."

With this last statement, Milly's eyes filled with tears, but Taylor rolled his eyes in response.

"You feel angry. Most of all, you feel sorrow."

"And *you* don't, Dad?" Taylor's emphasis expressed his disbelief.

"At first I felt physical pain, like someone punching the breath out of me, Taylor. Then shock. Later, I felt numb."

It suddenly became clear to both Milly and Taylor that their Dad was referring to his reactions after the wreck and the loss of his wife.

"Next, grief dug deeper than I had ever experienced. I tried to stay strong for you kids, but I couldn't shake the bad memories or the guilt that I, in one night, had ended the world we enjoyed as a family."

"But it wasn't your fault, Dad," Taylor declared. "It was Kailynn's fault."

"No, Taylor. It wasn't Kailynn's fault. And it wasn't my fault either. The road was slick with ice. Both cars started sliding about the same time. I checked it out. But even if she or I had caused the wreck, it would've been an accident. Kailynn could have gone over the ridge onto the railroad tracks, too. Don't you see that?" Beads of perspiration broke out on his forehead. "I shudder to think what would have happened if she and R.L. hadn't been there that night. You may have lost both parents."

They could only stare at him as the realization struck them.

"I have a confession to make to you kids. I've confessed it to God though He already knew it."

For a few minutes, the room was uncomfortably quiet while he considered how to tell them about this troubled time without influencing them to share its misery.

"I finally felt angry, not at a person, but at God for letting the wreck happen and taking Emma from me. She and I loved and served Him long before we met, and then in our marriage together. Suddenly, she was gone. My kids were motherless. I no longer had a voice to sing His praises or spread His word. So, I turned against Him for months. I didn't care about a book shop which exalted Him. I didn't know what I would do, but I wanted to let it go."

Milly's eyes rounded, and Taylor's face set with concern for his dad.

"About the time Kailynn appeared at the store I remembered Job, and how he had lost more than I did. I confessed my anger to God, but still didn't know how to pick up my life again."

Seeing the expressions on their faces, he wondered if he had done the right thing in telling them about his anger toward God. "I'm sorry to unload on you two, but I want to let you know that I understand your feelings. I'm sorry I put off crying too long. I admit I thought it was a sign of weakness, and by acting stoic I was being strong for you."

At this point he started to rise from the chair. "I needed to remember that Emma is more alive now than she would ever be on Earth."

"But I miss her here, Daddy." Milly's tears overflowed.

He sat back down. "I understand, Honey, but your mother wouldn't want you to spend the rest of your life grieving for her as if she were buried in that body in the ground."

"I loved her body," Milly choked.

"I know, Sweetheart, but her spirit isn't there anymore. Remember what Paul in the New Testament said? To be absent from the body is to be present with the Lord. Your mother is alive, well and happy. She would want you to be well and happy, too. Because of what our Savior went through on the cross, died and rose you will someday see your mother again. Think what a glorious and happy day that will be!"

Milly wiped her face with her hands and nodded. She slipped from the bed and into his arms. Hugging him tightly, she whispered, "I love you, Daddy."

Tears escaped his eyes. "I love you, too, Pumpkin."

Milly pulled back and looked into his eyes. "Now I have to take care of you."

"Yes, and I need to take care of you and Taylor."

They smiled into each other's tear-stained face.

~ ~ ~

Feeling restless, Rod decided to go into his studio to draw or paint when the telephone began to ring. Looking over his art materials he answered, "Hello."

A voice like Emma's said, "Please come and join me."

At first, he couldn't move his lips or find his voice. Suddenly, he came to his senses. "Who is this? Why are you doing this to me?" He saw that the caller ID was UNKNOWN as usual before the line went dead.

Hearing the delicate tinkle of wind-chimes outside, he walked to the side window near the back of the room. He remembered he had taken down every one of Emma's wind-chimes only a week after her death because he could no longer stand to hear them without his heart aching to also hear her voice. With the small lights installed around the house he could make out the form of a woman dressed in yellow slowly ascending the hill. He ran as quietly as possible so he wouldn't wake the children, taking the stairs two at a time. Hurrying out the kitchen door, he caught a glimpse of the woman dressed in yellow nearing the top of the hill. His voice came out in a whisper. "Emma?"

He garnered as much force as he could muster. "Emma!"

The woman suddenly disappeared out of his sight.

He reasoned that the beams from the small lights would only shine a few feet. Mystified, he put one foot in front of the other, moving up the knoll as stealthily as he could manage. By the time he reached the top he saw no one. He felt like a fool. *What's wrong with me? It couldn't possibly be Emma. Then who is it? Am I imagining the whole thing?* He wiped the perspiration above his upper lip and off his forehead with the back of his hand. Staying on the hill for a while, he took deep breaths and prayed as he looked into the night sky.

~   ~   ~

When she stepped upon the porch at home, Kailynn turned to say goodnight. Taking her hand in his, Joey, still standing on the top step, spoke tenderly, "Pray about something for the next few weeks, Kailynn."

"Certainly. What is it?"

"Consider marriage to me. Pray, and I will pray."

"Oh, Joey, it's too soon for me to consider marriage." She was amused by his arched brows. "I don't mean my age. Our friendship is new. We don't know each other that well."

"We already seem suited for each other, Kailynn."

Suited, she thought. *That is true in some sense and the same words Mother used. Is marriage to Joey God's will? How will I know? Because we are so suited? Or will God make His plans clearer?"*

"You promised to pray, Kailynn, when you didn't know what I was talking about."

"Yes, I did, Joey. And I will pray about marriage, but I don't make any promises until God shows us the right path to take."

"Fair enough. That's what I want, too." He pulled her forward, and she allowed a kiss on her cheek.

She stood on the porch for a while when he had gone, letting the scent of lilacs flood her senses. What was missing?

Her physical life was whole, her spiritual life was wonderful, and she had a good-looking godly young man practically propose marriage. *Why do I feel incomplete? What is missing?* She would surely pray longer tonight.

CHAPTER SIXTEEN

Milly tossed and turned, kicking back the pink sheet and multi-colored comforter. She stared up at the ceiling's swirling designs in the plaster and the pink and white fan. The light from the streetlamp cast shadowy leaf patterns across the walls and illuminated her framed pictures of ballerinas. She imagined that the smiles on the dancers' faces mocked her sadness.

Wonder if Tay is still up playing games. Maybe, he would stop long enough to talk to me.

She threw the remaining covers back so far they landed on the carpeted floor, but she walked as if she were sleeping, opened the door of her room and moved stealthily down the hall. On opening Taylor's door she felt disappointed when he wasn't sitting in front of his computer; and then alarmed when she saw his bed was empty and still made.

"Tay?" she whispered, trying not to wake her Dad.

"What ya want, Mill?"

His voice startled her. He was sitting in the computer chair in the corner of the room gazing toward the light of the screen saver displaying the star system.

"What's wrong, Taylor? Why are you sitting so still in the dark looking at those lights?"

"No reason."

"I know better than that, Tay."

Something about her manner reminded Taylor of his mother. "I feel bad about Kailynn and everything that's happened. Wish we could do a rewind and go back and change the way I acted the last day she was here."

"That's what I wanted to talk to you about."

"We can't change it, Mill. What's done is done."

"No, but maybe we can change the way things are now."

"And how do you plan to do that, Short Stuff?"

"We could call her and apologize, Tay."

"When? Couldn't call tonight. It's late"

"Why not? She probably can't sleep either. Come on, Tay. It's worth a try."

His voice cracked and then wailed, "Well, I'm not calling her!"

"Shhh… OK. I'll call, but you get on another phone and listen!"

He nodded.

~   ~   ~

In the middle of the night the telephone rang; and Kailynn flung the blankets back as she jumped up to run to answer in the living room before the insistent ringing could wake her parents.

"Hello…" she whispered, breathlessly waiting to hear who could be on the other end of the line.

A sweet, familiar voice responded, "Kailynn?"

"Milly? Is this you?"

"Yes. Taylor just picked up on the other phone downstairs."

"Is anything wrong, Milly?"

"Everything's wrong. And we don't know how to fix it."

"Honey, could you explain a little?"

"Taylor and I miss you. We don't know if we will all be together again.

"Where is your dad? Does he know you are still up and calling me?"

"No, he doesn't know. He's standing on the hill looking at the sky. He misses you, too."

"Did he say that?"

"No, but he paces up and down; and Stewart is going crazy following him.

Kailynn smiled sadly, especially when Milly added, "We think he's on the hill praying you will forgive us and come back."

"Honey, I do forgive any unkind words. I understand your reactions. I hope you forgive me for not telling you my terrible ordeal." Kailynn took a deep breath for her next words. "As for coming back there, your dad hasn't called me; and I think it best to disappear from your lives so you can move on." She heard gasps through both their phones before she had a chance to continue. "I will always love both you and Taylor. You are very special to me; and the three of you have taught me a lot."

"Oh no, Kailynn-" Milly's voice caught with emotion. "We love you, too. Don't we, Taylor?" At that, there was a click on the other phone. "We do, Kailynn. We are just hurting, but we both love you."

"I believe you, Honey. Now you'd better go on to bed. Pray to your Heavenly Father. Remember Jesus is a friend who never leaves you."

"I will..." Tears flooded the sound of her voice. "Goodbye, Kailynn."

"Goodnight, Sweetheart."

Kailynn placed the phone on the charger. She walked slowly into her bedroom, her fingers pressed together over her lips. Taking them down in resignation, she grasped her pillow, pulling it close to her stomach as she curled her body into a ball. She squeezed her eyes shut, but tears escaped down her cheeks.

The next day, everyone worked a little more subdued when Rod entered the shop two hours after Joey had led their morning prayer. He glanced in Kailynn's direction and spoke a soft good morning into the air for everyone in general. He closed the office door behind him. When it was time for the shop to close, he emerged with a dark countenance. "Sara, could I ask you to stay over for one more hour?"

"Sure. No problem. What's up?"

"Could you file a few papers I stacked on the filing cabinet in the office?"

Sara looked curious because he usually preferred to file his own papers or asked Kailynn. "Sure thing, Mr. Webster."

Joey had left at five o'clock for a two hour drive to a revival, saying a quick goodbye to Kailynn. Overhearing Rod requesting Sara to help him, she walked beyond the office to the back hall to hang up her smock. As she straightened her peach sun-backed dress and started to pick up her purse from a nearby table, Rod's shadow in the dim light fell across her.

"Could I speak to you for a few minutes, Kailynn?"

She recognized the paper he was holding in his hand as her resignation. "Yes, of course."

"You don't have to do this." He thrust the notice in her face.

"I feel I must under the circumstances."

"What circumstances? You are not responsible for the sorrows we suffered."

"I could have been the cause of the wreck."

"You could have been, but you weren't. Even if it were so, it would have been an accident as R.L. said. You could have been injured or killed as well." He paused and swallowed. "It's a miracle your heart stood the strain."

Tears rimmed her eyes. "The children turned away from me."

"Milly's heart is broken. She thinks she has lost her dearest friend."

"And Taylor?" her voice was a whisper.

"Taylor is remorseful, but he doesn't know how to face you, or what to do about it. He now understands his anger at the loss of his mother was misdirected at you."

"I care about them both, Rod; and I will talk with them." She steeled herself. "But I would only bring back unhappy memories every time they see me. It's best we all go on with our lives...separately."

Rod was quiet. She could feel more than see his eyes trying to penetrate her thoughts. She started to move around.

"Kailynn, are you and Joey serious?"

She paused. "He asked me to think about marriage."

"Do you love him?"

"I love a lot of things about him."

"Sounds like a great friendship."

"There's a great deal to love about Joey."

Rod threw the paper down, and grasped her shoulders firmly. "You are not in love with him, Kailynn, and we both know why."

"Don't, Rod." She shrugged away his hands, and he stepped aside.

Still not meeting his eyes, she touched his arm, but let her hand fall limply in a gesture expressing true resignation. Turning away, she willed herself through the store and out the door.

~ ~ ~

As soon as Carla came through the shop door a couple of weeks later, she realized it was a delivery day. Boxes were scattered in various places and invoices spread across the counter.

Sara was busy arranging new books in a display case. "Hi, Carla!" she greeted her with a cheerful smile.

Carla remembered the staff had been told to greet everyone who walked into the shop with cheerful words and smiles, but Sara's demeanor appeared genuinely friendly.

"Hello, Sara." She smiled in return with warmth and as much cheerfulness as she could muster, intent on the mission she was determined to accomplish. "Where is Rod?"

"In the back unboxing more new books. We are blessed with an abundant supply this time. They are beautiful, Carla, and I can see myself buying most of them. There goes another paycheck!"

Carla laughed as she moved past the counter. Approaching the hall, she heard Rod cutting tape. His back was to her, and she took a deep breath before calling his name.

He turned momentarily, but continued opening the small parcel perched on top of a stack of larger boxes. "Oh, hi Carla."

Where did the real Rod go? She wondered. *He is usually jovial when new books arrive. In the last few months he would generate happiness and the enthusiasm he and Emma had always shared when opening new devotionals, reference books and gift items. I'll start by feeling him out.*

"Where is Kailynn?"

He tossed the package aside and took hold of the next, larger box. "I wouldn't know. She isn't here anymore."

"She quit the store?"

"Yep." He grabbed the box cutter off the table, and started slashing through the cardboard."

"Uh, be careful, Mr. Webster. You don't want to cut into the merchandise."

He stopped, and turned toward her with a wry smile. His eyes looked tired and his frame weary.

"Could I talk with you privately for a few minutes, Rod?"

"Only if you want to talk about coming back to work here."

"No. I feel this job belongs to Kailynn."

"Well, you are wrong, my dear. She is gone."

Their eyes met, acknowledging the double meaning to that simple statement.

"Rod, can you tear yourself away from the store for a while and come outside to talk?"

"Guess I could use a break. Let's pick up coffee at the Coffee Shack and sit on one of the benches outside."

"Sounds good."

Once they had their Styrofoam cups in hand, he leaned back on the bench with the attitude that he didn't care if he ever rose from it again.

"Something has happened. Hasn't it, Rod?"

"Something I hadn't imagined would ever happen."

"I'm not talking about the car accident." At the change in her voice, he crooked his head and peered at her.

"You came here with an agenda today. Didn't you, Carla?"

She took a sip of her coffee before answering his question. "Not exactly. I'm just hoping you will explain what caused Kailynn to walk."

He looked away. "Is it any of your business?"

"Not unless you and Kailynn consider me a friend and not just an employee."

When he turned his head toward her his eyes and smile were warm. "Oh you know me too well."

"I want to understand the rift between you two. Hate to put you through it, and I don't wish to make you uncomfortable, Rod. Honestly, I don't. But please take the time to tell me what happened from your perspective."

Sitting up, he held his cup on his knees and began telling her about the happy beginning of that Spring day ending in shocking revelations and a torrent of tears.

"Did Kailynn quit immediately?"

"No, I guess the time and distance I put between us led her to that decision. But, Carla, I needed that time for my mind to process everything." He leaned back against the bench again. "Now she is gone. Gone from the store and gone from our lives. And it's my fault. I acted like a jerk."

"No, Rod. You behaved like someone who had suffered a tremendous loss and finally broke under the strain. It's okay to grieve. Jesus wept at Lazarus' tomb."

"But I crushed the joy out of my children, Carla. I can't forgive myself for that."

"No. The powers and principalities of the air did that for you. But hey, Rod, each day is a new opportunity to recreate good memories and allow God to restore what they have stolen."

"You're right, Carla. I'll talk to God about all of this and give Him a chance to work. Meantime, I'll take one day at a time and try to share His love with my kids." He sat up and gave her a look of curiosity. "Tell me something."

"If I can."

"Will she ever come back? Not just to the store but to our family?"

"I don't know. It depends on the three of you."

"The *three* of us?"

"Yeah. You, Kailynn and God."

"I guess you're right again. You really did read some of those books you sold, didn't you?" He gave her a broad smile.

She nodded, sensing she had completed her mission.

"Thank you, Carla. Thank you, my friend."

As she rose she reached out and patted his back. "See you, Rod."

In spite of his resolutions, the work hours dragged by for Rod. He felt his life was in limbo. A fatigue which had nothing to do with a lack of physical strength overwhelmed his mind. Tired of plodding along through his regular schedule, he decided to take a day off to try to recharge his energy level. Feeling unsettled when the only person he saw in the dining room was his own reflection in the windows as overcast skies made a dark background for the ceiling light's mirror image. He wondered why he had thought that lounging around in sweats could possibly make him feel better. He felt he had to do something or he would go out of his mind. Climbing the stairs he pondered his options, and then ran back down to find the key to his studio. The sight of the studio gave him a warm sensation, and the creative urge stirred in him. He put soft, instrumental music in the player, and carried a stretched canvas to the work table. Putting on his gloves he brushed primer over the surface, being sure to cover the sides. As he waited an hour for it to dry, he wondered what he would paint. He sat back, closing his eyes and letting the music saturate his mind. Visions of Kailynn appeared before his closed eyelids. Kailynn smiling in the sun; Kailynn startled, with a look of wonder lighting up her face; Kailynn laughing in the snow.

She is a refreshing flower garden after the rain. She is a ray of sunshine bursting through the clouds. She is the soft breeze lifting our spirits. Suddenly he knew what he wanted to paint. He wanted to express the way Kailynn made him feel. He would paint a flower garden glistening with raindrops, shimmering in shafts of sunlight.

Excited by the picture in his head and the joy in his heart, he applied the colors of oil paint he would need on his palette. Taking a two-inch brush, he used smooth strokes to spread the blue sky. With a fan brush he interloped circles to make his clouds, and then pulled them up with a one-inch brush. He stepped back to view and grinned at the thought of the next step. He took his palette knife and blended the colors he envisioned. Picking up a clean two-inch brush he began dotting clusters midway down the canvas. With another two-inch brush he mixed titanium white for some pastel blossoms.

For the stems and leaves, he twisted a small brush over and over in the mixture of cobalt blue and yellow with a little linseed oil, producing a stunning green. The creative juices flowed as he worked diligently on the rain drops and pulled down the shafts of light, smoothing them out over the existing colors. He reminded himself to step back to view, and know when to stop. When he did bring himself to stand at a distance to see if he had fulfilled his vision, he felt elated and satisfied.

CHAPTER SEVENTEEN

Needing to take a break from actively searching for a suitable job in which Kailynn could feel confident and use the abilities she had acquired while working at the bookstore, she stayed in her robe and went out onto the front porch of her home. Her Dad, freshly dressed in a blue checkered shirt and gray slacks, sat in one of the wicker armchairs, drinking coffee from his heavy brown mug. She eased into the other chair where her mother usually sat, slowly tipping a can of cola to her lips. At first, they sat in their comfortable and habitual silence – she staring out at the street, watching an occasional car go by; he, holding his mug chin-level with one hand, taking sips as he gazed at the distant treeline. What a comfort it was for her to sit with him again. She hadn't realized how much she had missed these quiet times.

Assuming a relaxed tone, and not looking in her direction, he inquired, "You're off work today?"

Still looking at the street, she replied, "Something like that."

This time, he peered at her out of the corner of his eye. "Oh? Did you decide to quit?"

Kailynn took an involuntary, deep breath. "Yes."

He turned to face her. "Any reason?"

Not wanting to hurt his feelings by ignoring the question or glancing away, she turned to him. "I can't stay at my first job forever. There comes a time when a person needs some space and an opportunity for growth."

"You mean, you need space between you and the Websters?" He lowered his head to look into her eyes.

With this, she couldn't bring herself to confess the truth. She had always wanted her dad to be proud of her. How could he have pride in her knowing everything she had done and not done? He would think she was manipulative. Maybe, unconsciously, she really was manipulative. Maybe she was as guilty as Agnes in thinking of self and attempting to control situations and people, even the people she loved most.

Her Dad rose from his seat and bent over to kiss her on the forehead. "It's going to be okay. It's all going to work out. You'll see."

She patted his arm tenderly, and gave him an affectionate smile.

In the early morning hours on Tuesday, Kailynn awoke to persistent shaking by her mother. "Get dressed, Honey. We have to take your Dad to the hospital."

She pulled on her gray slacks and matching jersey. She and Mae helped Lee to her car. Supporting his arm, she was shocked to feel his bones through his pajamas. Always lean, he had also been strong with hard muscles.

Once he was placed on a hospital bed, she noticed his drawn face and white hair. *When had he aged so much? When did he lose this much weight and why?*

"He hasn't been able to keep much food down," Mae informed the doctors.

"Has he complained of pain?" one of the doctors asked.

Mae frowned. "He's a quiet man, not one to complain, but I could tell he's been in pain for days now. He doesn't like to go to doctors."

A surgeon recommended surgery to see if he had a blockage. Kailynn and her dad looked at each other. *Can he endure an operation?* She knew her dad was wondering, too. *But if he does have a blockage, I could lose him.* "Maybe you'd better have surgery, Dad."

He looked from her face to Mae's, and then he nodded his head.

It seemed the longest time she had ever waited as she and her mother prayed together. When the surgeon approached them, he shook his head. "There wasn't a blockage. He's in intensive care, still sedated." He looked worriedly at Mae. Speaking to Kailynn, he continued. "There won't be any change until late morning. You should take your mother home.'

"Alright. Mother, let's go home and pray."

She and Mae peeped through the door at her father, lying white as the sheet tucked around him.

Later in the day, Kailynn and her mother were confused when he was not in the room where they had left him. Nurses told them the room number where he had been transferred. Finally, there, they wouldn't leave him until the doctor had checked him. He was cognizant though incredibly weak.

The doctor explained to Mae immediately, "We had to remove him from life support because we discovered you had signed a paper forbidding it."

Kailynn looked startled.

Mae wiped her eyes with a handkerchief. "Yes, we both agreed we wouldn't want to be on life support. I didn't know that meant right after surgery. I thought it was when someone was dying."

Joey arrived in the late evening before leaving out of town. Kailynn and her mother both were exhausted emotionally and physically since they dosed fitfully in the straight-back chairs. "I'd like nothing better than to stay with you, but I'm in the middle of a revival."

"No, Joey, you go ahead. God has given you a job to do. There's nothing you can do here. They're running more tests."

He gave her shoulders a squeeze; and then knelt beside Mae's chair, patting her wrinkled hand. She sat with her head drooping and an expression of sad acceptance of something secret only she sensed with a certainty. "Let me take your mother home, Kailynn. Her feet are beginning to swell."

Kailynn looked down at her mother's feet encased in the low, black pumps. There was swelling over the bridge of her feet and around the ankles. Pretty soon, she wouldn't be able to stand on them, let alone walk.

"Mother, please allow Joey to drive you home where you can rest. I'll stay until the patients are settled for the night."

With the young man's help her mother hobbled over to the hospital bed; and bent down to kiss her husband's brow, now turned upward toward the bridge of his nose in forbearance of great suffering.

As the night wore on, shadows rising across the walls of the hospital room, Kailynn noticed a trickle of blood escaping the corner of her father's mouth. She rang for assistance; and in only moments, watched as a nurse suctioned the blood out. The next time she observed blood strangling him, she steeled herself to suction him before the nurse entered the room. Soon, it became a routine, that and taking a sponge on a stick like some weird popsicle to moisten his lips and mouth. She and a few hospital personnel suspected liver failure though reports weren't available, yet. She was sitting in the far corner near the wide window staring toward the bed with its overhead lamp spotlighting her dad's stoic features. Girlhood memories rolled by her mental vision as thunder rumbled in the distance and raindrops pelted the window. Memories of her dad helping her with math problems; presenting to her delightful mystery books or happily-ever-after romances or sharing his favorite geography or history texts. He would run his hands over the spine of the books, instructing her to take good care of them, even to number them the way he did his own volumes. She remembered him playing checkers with her or Chinese checkers, with their smooth marbles fitting snugly into their appropriate holes. There were memories of strolls through flower gardens and walks under the stars while he explained about planets in the solar system. He had taken time with her whenever he wasn't at the chemical plant working or repairing something with his many tools around the house. She wished she had not been so swallowed up in her own problems, real and imagined, as she developed into a self-absorbed teenager, that she didn't take time to know him better.

She realized her dad had been a fascinating person, really; and as much as they had shared together, she had missed out on so much more. She wanted to ask him to tell her more about the years when he was young. She would insist he teach her chess and to play the guitar – the two things she always thought she would learn. Funny, her weakened heart was frustrating yet she had never dwelt on the possibility of death, probably the hormonal blessing of teen years, though she knew many teens do think about it during those years. She could see now that her parents fought that old spirit of fear every day of their lives.

Kailynn's father had survived a POW camp in Vietnam, coming home with scars from hooks, but nevertheless whole. He and his wife would wait some time to make a home; and after losing one child in utero, raise a daughter whose life depended on the next heartbeat. *But don't we all depend on that precious heartbeat we take for granted,* she reminded herself. *How tenuous. We are at the mercy of God. What really mattered,* she concluded, *was whether or not our heart is right with God.*

A figure filling the doorway and a rustling movement toward the lamp brought Kailynn out of her reverie. Agnes' red hair lit up the room along with the lamplight. Her eyes searched the room for Kailynn. "Is he conscious?"

"Yes, he's just sleeping. I think they're giving him morphine. His face seems more relaxed."

Agnes also took a seat farther in the corner where she could talk privately to Kailynn. "Don't you need to go home and freshen up? Maybe eat and rest even if you return before morning? I'd be glad to stay with him."

"Thanks, Agnes, but I'm not ready to leave yet."

Suddenly, Rod stood near her chair. "At least, come down to the cafeteria and grab a bite." He put out a hand.

Agnes urged her to go. "I'll stay with your dad, Honey. I'm quite qualified," she stated, as a matter of fact, but an ironic sadness lifted the corners of her mouth in a poignant smile.

Kailynn agreed, letting Rod help her rise from her chair. She would choose a few food items easily picked at and bring black coffee back to the room.

Afterward, the three discussed her father's condition in low tones. He stirred in the bed emitting strong moans a few times. When Kailynn leaned over the bed, his eyes were open and he mouthed urgently, "Have faith in God."

Did he not like the negative parts of the discussion? Was he asking her to have faith he would come out of this physical condition, or to keep faith in God in spite of it?

When Rod stood at the bed, Lee reached for his hand and squeezed it. "Help me die."

Rod looked into his eyes and nodded agreement, too choked by emotion to speak.

When Agnes left, Rod remained seated in the corner. Kailynn couldn't object or encourage him to leave because her father had asked him to be with him, a weighty request so simply stated: *Help me die.*

~   ~   ~

The next morning, Joey brought Mae to see her husband. She hobbled on her still swollen feet toward the left side of the bed, smoothed the sheets around Lee's chest and held his hand with both of hers. She wanted to kiss him but his bed was rolled too high, so she kissed his hand instead. Her eyes looked deeply into his tortured gaze.

He made an effort to whisper, "My r...ring..."

Mae pulled the golden band over his knuckle, holding it tenderly with shaking fingers. "You'd better sleep now, Lee," she whispered back in a permissive tone.

His grip tightened. "I love you," he mouthed.

"I'll always love you, too, Lee. For...ever..."

He relaxed his hand and smiled. "I...I'll sleep now."

Her tears dropped onto their interlocked fingers. "See you in the morning."

He squeezed her hand one last time, then looked steadily ahead while she turned away, needing Joey's arm to lean on as she hobbled through the doorway.

Kailynn hurried out into the hall to caress her mother who stood still, but whose mind and heart were too full of memories and unspoken meanings to respond. The daughter walked to the end of the corridor when they had descended on the elevator. There she watched out the window, trying to keep her composure and her resolve to stay strong for both parents, when she caught sight of the back of a familiar vehicle, moving slowly through the rain. The taillights glowed red as it slowed to a stop. She recognized it as her dad's car – the car he would never drive again. She could see him in her mind sitting in his dignified posture. Wearing his brown leather jacket and his brown hat firmly perched on his head, he handled the steering wheel with purpose. Like a dam bursting, tears flooded her face as sobs wracked her body. Strong arms surrounded her collapsing frame, and steady hands loosed the clip and stroked her hair, drawing her head to his shoulder. Her weak legs found support when Rod lifted her body onto the leather sofa in front of the window and let her cry out the pain, her arms clinging to him as they dared not cling to her father.

When she felt drained of emotion and tears, she began apologizing. "I'm sorry, I don't know why I'm losing control."

He handed her a box of tissues from a nearby table. "I do. This is what I experienced that day in the living room. Because of the children, I had never allowed myself to cry. I'm sorry you felt at fault because I held back so much hurt."

She wiped her face with the tissues. Knowing, without a mirror, her appearance displayed how distraught she felt. She gazed up at him.

"I'm here for you, Kailynn, not to take advantage of this moment of heartache, but as your friend." His speech impediment, hardly noticeable until now, became more pronounced but wonderfully comforting to her. "I'll stand by your father because he asked me, and I'm standing by you for as long as you need me."

She relaxed against him; relieved she could trust his friendship and didn't have to think of anything other than these too few precious hours with her dad.

As it turned out, Rod wasn't in the room when the time came for Lee to leave this earth. As midnight approached, he had dropped off to sleep in the tall corner chair after persuading Kailynn to lie across the other bed. When a nurse padded into the room to check the IV, Kailynn sat up to observe her every move.

"When do *you* sleep?" the nurse asked.

"I don't yet," Kailynn replied flatly. "I can sleep later."

The nurse stopped in the doorway as though she would like to say something, but what was there to say? They both knew it was futile to suggest sleep to Kailynn.

By daybreak, she rose, determined to send Rod home to shower, shave and eat breakfast with his children.

"No, I promised your dad I'd be here."

"You need to go and -"

"No...n...oh...oh...," her dad's voice groaned from the bed, but his eyes were half shut when they turned to look. Was he objecting to her decision, bewailing Rod's possible departure or groaning in pain? Surely, it was his physical deterioration.

"We'll be okay until you return," she insisted. "You need to freshen up and check on the kids."

"Well, promise me you'll eat when they bring the tray to you."

"Sure. I could really use some coffee."

He gave her a hug and rushed out the door with the intention of taking only the minutes necessary to accomplish the personal needs.

Soon someone set the breakfast tray beside the chair at the foot of the patient's bed, where she had sunk immobile since Rod left, somehow glad to be alone with her dad. The first item she saw was the cup of black coffee; and she reached for it with both hands. Strangely, a white card glistened underneath the saucer as she lifted it. She placed the coffee on the tray, and sat looking at the black letters until the sentence registered in her brain: "If you love me, you would want me to go to the Father..." She didn't read the rest of the scripture or the reference. She instinctively knew - as deeply as her mother had sensed - that whenever she would raise her eyes, her dad would be going home. She read the words again, *Go to the Father.* She lifted her eyes. His head was tilted slightly to the right, a sad expression in his eyes as he gazed across the room at his daughter. Blood trickled down the corners of his mouth.

She stood as if in a dream; and walked to the front desk right outside his room. A nurse looked up questioningly. "My dad is dying now."

The nurse copped a superior attitude and slowly entered the room. As soon as she saw the patient, she ran back for a stethoscope. Another nurse helped to check him. Kailynn stood beside her dad, holding his left hand as he had often held her little hand when crossing a busy intersection on the way to purchase their beloved books. She felt life in his hand even though it lay motionless. When they stopped checking him, she said, "It's alright, Dad. Don't be afraid. Go on. It's alright." His hand gradually went completely limp.

One of the nurses said, "Lower the bed. Let her hug him."

When the bed lowered, Kailynn walked to the right side and put her arms around her dad, and held him close. A peace enveloped her own soul as she noticed his arched brows were smooth again, his battle over.

CHAPTER EIGHTEEN

Relatives, friends, former enemies who through years and familiarity had formed a bond with the Richardson family, church members whose association made them feel like part of the family and even Mayor Morris attended the wake, and now the funeral. Mae sat on the front row flanked by Kailynn on one side and Joey on the other with her three gray-headed sisters seated at the end of the pew. She chose to wear a blue suit; and her daughter, a long silver dress with a little black jacket. Kailynn's spirit actually brightened when she saw Agnes wearing a red suit, knowing her new sister in Christ believed in eternal life. She shook her head and smiled to think that in the past she would have resented Rod's neighbor for daring to wear red to her father's funeral, and would surely have taken the suit as a disgraceful expression of disrespect. Today she understood Agnes' choice. She was making a vivid statement to the fact that Kailynn's father was more alive now than he had ever been.

Mae's eyes misted over at moments; other times, they gazed out into the room, viewing memories instead of her immediate surroundings. She did focus as a friend and former pastor, Reverend Gerald Hoff spoke about her husband's desire for peace. Throughout the message, he called him a peacemaker and a man of peace. She paid attention, too, as Joey rose and stepped up to the podium to sing of a home in heaven and a celestial land where they would all be reunited.

As people filed by to pay their respects before viewing the coffin, Rod, Taylor, and Milly stepped from the back of the room. While Rod held Mae's hand, she looked up at him in silence, seeing in his eyes that he empathized with her loss even in the midst of her faith. She took her hands and placed his in her daughter's, giving a squeeze as though blessing them. Surprised, Kailynn looked around at Mae's face and then up at Rod as he kept his composure.

"We're praying for both of you, Kailynn."

Still looking into his eyes, she nodded.

Taylor patted her shoulder; and Milly hugged her gently.

Kailynn spent the following days helping Mae pack Lee's belongings in boxes. His desk proved the hardest for her emotionally and yet somehow warming as she rediscovered her childhood reports and essays. She handled his mechanical pencils inscribed with his name lovingly, deciding to keep them in her room. Her pain was softened by precious memories.

It seemed to help her mother to take telephone calls, finally talking about their hospital experience and her loss. During the meal which neighbors and the church brought after the funeral, she had talked quietly of other trivial matters, but now felt a release by expressing her pain. There were times her words were noticeably tinged with anger, but those moments passed quickly and good memories replaced them.

Suddenly, Kailynn found herself sitting on the porch swing staring up at the mountainous skyline darkening in the twilight. The stars gradually appeared as bright as diamonds; and yet, she didn't stir even to pull her long beige cardigan together over her blue cotton blouse. When she shifted her vision to the full moon, she yearned for Rod to view the celestial display too. She thought of calling his house, but such action would probably disrupt this much needed peaceful pause in the midst of her own pain. Besides, was she confusing loneliness with love?

CHAPTER NINETEEN

Rod stood still on the knoll, a dark silhouette in jersey and jeans, watching the stars appearing over the mountains. *One forgets that the full moon and bright stars in the children's books are only attempts to illustrate the nightly display in the sky,* he thought. *When did we stop looking up into the sky and admiring God's handiwork? At a certain age? When life's circumstances kept us on the run until we fell into bed, glad to sleep? Time to stop and take stock of my life. Things were getting back to normal. No! Not normal. Not that. But we, the children and I were living again. Actually looking forward to each day. Instead of dreading the day, we were waking up to plans. Kailynn brought out the best in the kids, almost as if she could see into their personalities, see through their eyes. She seemed to have an innate ability to understand my situation, too. I wouldn't admit it, and she didn't say it, but I felt love flow from her.*

In turn, love stirred in my heart. Now, she obviously feels rejected, and refuses to take a risk of another hurtful episode. Lord, there has to be some way to make her see how much she means to each of us. Surely, she could sense the unbelievable shock, the guilt, the initial self loathing, and the grief I had finally permitted myself to express. Has my anger cost me the one person who God had inspired to help us start living each day to the fullest? What do I do now, God? Show me how to bring light into Kailynn's eyes again, a smile of joy and a look of wonder to her face.

He suddenly understood what he had to do, no matter what anyone else decided or the consequences. He strode purposefully into the living room, and hesitated only a couple of seconds as he looked at Emma's portrait he had painted with love. Reaching up both hands, he took it down from the wall. Emma wouldn't want enshrined instead of Christ. She wouldn't want to be the focus and center of the family. Not now that she had gone to the Father. He carried it upstairs; and hung it in the alcove between the children's rooms. They could place fresh flowers on the table below it whenever they wanted.

For now, he hung his painting of the flower garden above the mantle. The next thing he did was to call Joey.

"Hello, Joey. Do you think you could come over for coffee and a talk?"

"Tonight?"

"Yes. The sooner the better. It's kind of important to me. We need to get something straight."

After starting coffee brewing in the kitchen, Rod moved outside to wait for Joey, and rehearse mentally what he needed to say to his longtime friend and now coworker.

"Hey, Buddy, what's up?" Joey's low tone of voice and serious facial expression interrupted his thoughts.

Joey knew by his determined manner that Rod had come to some kind of irreversible decision. With a coffee mug in hand, the first thing Joey noticed on taking a seat in the living room was the new painting gracing the fireplace. His vision took in the garden scene before looking into Rod's steady stare.

"Do you plan to marry Kailynn?" Rod's voice sounded oddly stronger.

The direct question took Joey off guard. He didn't want to have this conversation with his best friend, and lowered his eyes from Rod's penetrating blue scrutiny. His white tailored shirt and navy blue jacket felt stiff; and he squirmed trying to relax. "I've asked her to marry me."

"Do you love her?"

"I love many things about her. I think she would develop into a good wife in ministry."

"That's funny. She said the same thing about you." Seeing the puzzled look on his friend's face, he added, "That she loved many things about you." Rod paused before going on to ask, "But are you in love with her?"

Joey raised his eyes at this question. "You mean, is she on my mind twenty-four hours and do I desire her above all other women? That will come in time."

Rod's eyelids closed at this answer. His left hand held the mug while his right hand fingered the rim of the cup. "That's not good enough, Joey."

The younger man waited for an explanation to follow.

Finally, Rod met his stare. "I love Kailynn."

Joey ventured, "She *is* good with the children."

Impediment forgotten, Rod's voice sounded emphatic. "I'm *in love* with Kailynn."

For a moment, Joey shut his own eyes against this revelation. He sat perfectly still, considering the weight of these words.

~ ~ ~

Sara stopped dusting shelves, straightened the beret holding back the sides of her hair, pulled up the waistband of her black slacks and slipped her hands into the pockets of her blue smock. Puzzled, she looked at Joey sitting on the stool in front of the cash register, an elbow propped on the counter with the knuckle of his index finger rubbing his lower lip. She had never seen him this quiet and pensive. Her slippered feet itched to walk straight to his side, but a filter somewhere in her brain shot up red flags, and she controlled the impulse.

She finally approached the counter softly easing over to him. "Hey, a penny for your thoughts."

Lowering his arm, he worked his neck from side to side. Trying to grin, he said, "I don't need a penny. I need some answers."

"You? *You* need answers? The man with all the answers needs answers?"

He looked at her then, and pressed his lips together before speaking again. "You have a bloated image of me, Sara. I know the scriptures, but sometimes find it difficult to read people."

"Who do you want to read?"

When he didn't answer but gazed toward the plate glass window she added, "Kailynn?"

He inhaled through his nostrils and loosened the top of his white shirt.

She scrutinized his expression from the darkening eyes to the tight, serious set of his mouth.

"I'm ready to listen, Joey. Telling someone might make you feel better. Look, we all need someone we can bounce things off. How 'bout it?"

"I can't talk here."

"It's almost closing. Why don't we have dinner together at a place where we can talk as long as we want?"

"There is that new restaurant with tables outside near the river."

"Okay." She pivoted on her heels, picked up the feather duster and went to the front of the store to knock dust off the shelves and gift items before he could change his mind. She prayed she would have the grace to know when to listen and when and what to speak.

When they had arrived at the restaurant, chosen the buffet and settled at a white table near the river, Joey said the blessing over the food and they ate in silence for a few minutes. It was pleasant for both of them to watch the occasional boat passing the peacefully flowing Kanawha. A soft breeze brushed against their faces and tenderly touched the strands of hair.

"Are you feeling better now?" Sara initiated conversation.

"It feels good to be outside. It's a beautiful evening."

Sara put her fork down on her plate, and fingered the collar of her floral print blouse. "No, I mean, do you feel better about what was bothering you?"

Now it was his turn to put his fork down and reach for his soft drink hoping he wouldn't have to respond to this line of questioning.

She picked up her fork as if to resume eating, and then paused. "What happened, Joey? Remember we came here to talk about it."

"It?"

"Should I say *her*? Tell me what happened. Did it involve Rod?"

Picking his fork back up, he held it in his hand as if doing so would steady his voice. He decided to confide in Sara. He felt a need to talk to someone, and Sara was the most trustworthy woman he had ever met. He told her about the accident that took Emma out of their familiar world and the blow-up at the house; and finally, the conversation Rod and he had concerning Kailynn. When he had finished, he was surprised at how effortlessly he had recalled it all in words.

Sara remained quiet the whole time he spoke, only the expression in her eyes giving him the sense that she understood and the encouragement to follow through to the end. She waited until she was sure he was completely through describing the events on his mind, before saying anything. When he began picking at his food again, she shocked him by asking, "Well, *do* you love her?"

He put his fork down again with a clatter as he rolled his eyes and gesticulated broadly with his hands. "Why does everyone ask if I love her?"

She merely looked at him, waiting for an answer.

"As I have said many times, I love her personality and traits. What is there not to love about Kailynn?"

"I mean, are you *in love* with her?"

"Now *you* sound like Rod. What does that mean anyway? Either you love someone or you don't. *You* want bells and whistles. There's more to love than being starry-eyed over someone. What if I constantly asked you if you love me? Your mind immediately runs and makes a list of all the things you appreciate about me. Let's see now. Do you love me?"

Her fork clicked against the plate as she quickly lowered her eyelids. "This isn't about me."

A pause in conversation took place as they went back to eating and looking out toward the river.

Setting her glass of ice tea on the table after taking a sip, Sara spoke first. "Loving lots of things about a person is the reason for a great friendship, not a marriage, Joey."

"My word, you sound like Rod!"

"It's just the truth, Joey. Many a good friendship has been ruined when the couple mistakenly marries. In time, the marriage disintegrates and ends in divorce."

He flinched when he imagined this scenario.

"You need to give Kailynn and Rod a break. It's apparent they are in love, and need time and space to work it out."

She stated the obvious so simply he couldn't miss it.

"You'll find the woman who will complete your life if that is what you desire when God brings her to you. You will fall in love with her as much as you develop an appreciation for her ways." Taking a deep breath, she continued. "Wait upon the Lord, Joey. That is what I am doing; and that's my advice to you."

He suddenly smiled his toothy Joey smile in her direction as if a weight had suddenly fallen from his shoulders.

"You are a surprisingly wise woman, Sara. Quite an encourager. That's an extraordinary gift, my dear."

She smiled too, her eyes glistening in the twilight. "Thank the Lord."

CHAPTER TWENTY

Exasperated, Kailynn inclined her head toward the window of the city bus. Dressed in a royal blue suit with her hair swept up in a knot, she had tracked job openings across Charleston. One of the best paying office positions had brought her into confrontation with a jerk of a boss.

"Where have you worked?" he had inquired, though looking at her application.

"A Christian bookstore."

"What did you do? Clerking?"

"That and read to children."

"Huh, huh," he uttered. What do you plan to do?"

"Work and perhaps take more college courses."

"Oh, no. I don't want some goody-two-shoes making trouble for my girls. They get along fine, and none of them have a college education."

"Well, have a good day anyway." She fled the interview with much relief. Her throat dry, she drank thirstily from the water fountain before leaving the building.

The bookstores where she had applied were not looking for new employees. She took note, though, that the warmth and excitement generated by Rod's store was missing, or had she missed Rod and the other co-workers? Working in another bookstore owned and operated by someone else would have made her feel sad. *I miss him. I miss everything about him. It's not just loneliness because I have friends like Joey.* Thinking of Rod's life, it suddenly occurred to her that if it was only a matter of familiarity and a need to complete his family, he could have responded to Agnes months ago. "Oh, Lord, I miss him so much!" She startled herself by speaking aloud. She looked around to see if anyone appeared to have heard, but men and women who sat back in their seats seemed to be caught up in their own thoughts as they looked either straight ahead, out the windows, or on their phones.

When she arrived home, she headed for her room without supper. Propping herself up on the bed with the back of her head against the headboard, she felt overwhelmed with the pain in her heart. A different kind of pain. This pain was not physical, but it was an ache of such magnitude she could hardly bear the weight of it. Often frustrated with restrictions through her childhood and teen years, she had never known, never experienced such deep hurt. It was almost as if another person she loved had died, only worse. This person, *these people,* she had learned to love were living but dead *to her.* She fought her emotions, but her chin quivered. She squeezed her eyes shut, but tears escaped, flooding her whole face, when sobs tore out of her chest on their way to God as cries for help and a plea for mercy. For a while, she let all the hurt out until she felt broken and empty. Reaching for her Bible on the nightstand, she wiped her eyes with the back of her other hand. She sought scriptures to help her fill up the void left in her heart. *What scriptures can do that, Lord? Holy Spirit, our Comforter, show them to me. I need them so much now, just as much as a drowning man needs a life-raft.* Suddenly, scriptures stood out as she leafed through the pages, looking for sections about loss. *I will cling to words of comfort and strength as that drowning man clings to a liferaft or inner-tube!*

She read the words of Jesus first in John 14:16 and 17. "And I will pray the Father, and he shall give you another Comforter, that he may abide with you forever;

Even the Spirit of truth; whom the world cannot receive, because it seeth him not, neither knoweth him: but ye know him; for he dwelleth with you, and shall be in you." Psalm 147:3 spoke to her. "He healeth the broken in heart and bindeth up their wounds." *Yes,* she thought, I *feel wounded, full of wounds, but God can bind up those wounds if I let Him. I don't know how, but He knows how.* She remembered Romans 8:28 and turned there: "And we know that all things work together for good to them that love God, to them who are the called according to his purpose." *Lord, I know you can take the hurt we are all experiencing and turn it into healing. You can take this mess and transform it into a message of hope and peace. I know I can't depend on my feelings, so please forgive me if I feel a little empty right now. I do trust You with my life.*

The telephone rang; and her mother called from the kitchen, "Can you get that, Kailynn?"

Kicking her high heels off, she answered, "Hello." Her voice sounded hollow even in her own ears.

"Hello, Kailynn," Joey greeted her in a strained voice. "Could you come to Rod's church with me Sunday evening?"

"I suppose."

"What's wrong?"

"Oh, nothing. I just had the most ridiculous day job hunting. I'll talk with you later."

~ ~ ~

Several people dotted the pews on both sides of the aisle when Joey and Kailynn entered the church Sunday. The evening was comfortably warm; and the shaded lights overhead in the sanctuary glowed softly. The brightest light shone amber hues over the pulpit and the piano. The smell of lemon polish and a scent of fresh flowers on the communion table heightened their senses. As they sat down, a dozen more people slipped quietly into their seats. The atmosphere enveloped them with a feeling of peace and reverence as they sat looking at the cross over the baptistery, each in private meditation.

Sara, in a long blue cotton dress, approached the piano, glancing back toward Joey when he rose and slowly walked toward her. He was a handsome figure in his dark blue suit. They spoke in low tones. Taking the place behind the pulpit he announced the page number for the first hymn, and led the group in *Oh How I love Jesus*, and then, *Jesus Is The Sweetest Name I Know*. The words they sang helped their minds to focus on the Person Who loved so deeply He gave His life to save the lost.

An expectant silence filled the room when it was time for special music. The bulletin didn't list anyone. Everyone assumed Joey would sing with recorded music. Joey's eyes scanned the gathering. "We are in for a treat tonight. Rod asks for you to pray for him as he sings *In The Garden.*

The microphones picked up a gasp near the front. Turning around in her seat, Agnes' big smile and waving hands coaxed everyone in applause. Kailynn's right hand touched the collar of her white blouse in reflex as she watched Rod rise from the front pew, his back straight in his brown suit. She thought he would never turn that noble profile to face them.

The pause seemed interminably long as he whispered to Sara. He stood finally near the piano, microphone in hand, his suit jacket unbuttoned, his tieless white shirt open at the throat. It was soon apparent that he was envisioning another scene entirely. His raspy voice began to sing softly with the first notes. The sound carried an intimate quality while he sang of meeting the Lord in the garden when dew sparkled on the roses, walking and talking with Him. On the higher notes, his voice grabbed at each heart with its strained, heartbreaking sound of honest emotion. His blue eyes gleamed, and love overflowed his words. Waves of awe washed over his listeners. Everyone sat mesmerized by the vision of a personal relationship with God. Clapping cascaded throughout the room. Rod stepped down to meet Joey's handshake and pats on the back.

"Let's talk about trusting the Lord tonight," Joey announced from the pulpit. "Let's talk about whether the Lord can trust *you*!" Kailynn realized he was the one preaching this evening; and focused her attention from Rod to him, ready to turn to the scriptures in her Bible which lay open on her white linen skirt. At the end of his message, he asked them if they could walk and talk with God through the day as in Rod's song. After he led all of them to sing the refrain together, he asked if anyone wanted to come to the altar to ask God for a closer walk, to surrender their life and learn to trust Him more, to make Him Lord of their life. While others made their way forward to bow down, Kailynn knelt at the altar, praying for guidance.

In the line to exit the sanctuary, she saw the two men standing by the door shaking hands. Though she stepped aside to wait for Joey, she suddenly looked into Rod's face. *That dear face,* she thought. Then, feeling like he might read her mind, she looked away as if seeking out Joey. Rod didn't move; and his presence commanded her attention. Again she looked him full in the face, taking in the broad forehead, the vivid blue eyes, the handsome nose and the strong chin with its cleft. Their eyes locked.

"Come back, Kailynn," he said wistfully. "Come back to the store. We need you."

She couldn't help wondering if his words conveyed a double meaning, spoken in such a wistful manner.

"No strings attached. I promise." His lips tightened in a straight line and his eyes darkened in earnestness.

The bookstore is the place where God had led her; the place where she found her niche; the place where she felt appreciated. Still gazing into his face, she nodded her head in agreement.

Joey gazed on the two of them with a sad countenance dissolving into an expression of compassion. As Kailynn exited, he led her by the elbow out the door. In the car, he turned to face her. "Kailynn, I know I asked you to make a promise before you knew I was asking you to pray about marriage. I don't think I should hold you to that promise."

"You are such a good friend to my family, Joey." She put her hand on his arm. "I don't want to lose your friendship."

"That will never happen."

"Thank you."

~   ~   ~

Joy leaped up in her heart when Kailynn entered the bookstore her first day back. A happy assurance flooded her mind. This was the place where God wanted her to work. Surrounded by the inspiring books and gift items, energy coursed through her body. The satisfied expression on Rod's face as he nodded a greeting removed any shadow of doubt.

Sara bounded through the door in jeans and a *Jesus is Lord* tee-shirt. "Hey, Girl, it's about time you came back to work! I need a vacation too!"

Kailynn grinned. "Reporting for duty." She had worn her khaki slacks and shirt in expectation of boxing books.

Days passed pleasantly. She enjoyed the busy work of preparing books for delivery and dusting shelves. The boys and girls appeared delighted by her dramatic and expressive readings of the new books. Of course, each one wanted a copy of their own. She realized that she and the staff created memories every week.

When Sara took her vacation, Kailynn didn't offer to help with puppets, other than introducing the play. Rod managed to handle all the characters himself. It occurred to her after a while that Milly and Taylor never stopped in the store, and that Rod didn't mention them. As much as she wondered, she resisted the temptation to ask about them.

One day on her lunch break, she stood staring out the plate glass window at green leaves against a backdrop of blue sky. Contemporary praise music swelled through the store. Smoothing the light material of her yellow suit, she turned to catch Rod gazing across the counter in her direction. She detected the obvious effort with which he forced his vision to scan the invoice in his hand. She fought a desire to ask him to take a walk with her on this lovely day. "I'm taking a walk on my break, Rod."

"That's fine." Not looking up, his soft voice betrayed his composure.

She felt him watch her stroll down the walk. "Oh, what are we going to do, Rod? What a predicament we avoid!" A lady's look told her she had spoken aloud again. Feeling a headache coming on, she took out her clip and swung her hair around her shoulders as if shaking off her thoughts and losing them in the beauty of the day. Walking along the boulevard she felt as though her low heeled shoes sported little wings. *What a wonderful feeling! Is this the way everyone else always felt when they walked or did they take the effortless breaths for granted?* The sun glinted off the Capital's gold dome in the distance. Kailynn remembered that the people of West Virginia had insisted the gold remain as a symbol of mountaineer pride and hope. The Kanawha River sparkled as an occasional coal barge made its way slowly among the few houseboats moving up and down the water. The trees planted along the streets shimmered; their green leaves natural sun-catchers. Rhododendron nodded pink, purple or white blossoms with the soft breeze. Once in a while a flowerbed caught her attention. Old houses, some of them still homes, some housing businesses, delighted her with their grand architecture. As much as she found pleasure in the smooth, sleek lines of modern buildings, she was enraptured when light glistened on the windows of the refurbished, historic section in downtown Charleston, the eyes of rooms with stories of the past to tell.

She felt amazed at the number of blocks her feet covered in the allotted time. Instead of breathlessness, energy coursed through her body. Most of all, a healing in spirit as she prayed, prompted her to say aloud, "Thank You, Dear God, my ever present friend!"

When she walked into the store, Rod noticed the spark of vitality in her face, and sensed the renewal in spirit as she smiled freely in his direction. A ray of sunshine pierced his heart. *Are the two of us really ready to embrace life together? Can I finally be sure that love is not loneliness and longing for the past. Can she be sure, at last, that love is not a form of guilt or a longing to recompense? Do we need more time and prayer, with a certain understanding between us? Lord, would You reveal wisdom to her as well as to me?*

CHAPTER TWENTY-ONE

The first day Rod brought Taylor to the store to practice with new, large puppets, Kailynn greeted the teenager with, "Hey, Taylor."

"Hey." He sneaked a glance, and then avoided eye contact.

Genuine warmth filled her heart at the sight of him in blue jeans and gray t-shirt. One day she happened into the room when Rod and he were busy practicing a puppet play. The father's voice, soft but husky, almost blended with the background music. Taylor's big, strong looking puppet with spiked sandy-color hair spoke with a Hungarian accent. Humor rippled through her diaphragm and escaped in a sudden burst of mirth. Two heads popped up beside their puppets, their eyebrows raised in surprise. Broad grins rapidly stretched their features when they saw her start to laugh uncontrollably, just as they hoped the children would do. After that day, Taylor and Kailynn relaxed with each other. They usually joined Rod and Milly over sandwiches in the gazebo outside or at one of the tables in the story room on Children's Day. The boy's witty observations of the world around him made the young woman smile, and even laugh out loud at times. Milly, in colorful capris and pretty flowered tops, came only on that special day. She listened to the stories and worked on crafts. She talked about books and favorite authors, the puppet shows and her enjoyment of her creations. When they were all together, life seemed right and good. Contentment reflected on their faces as they talked.

~ ~ ~

On a Friday, Rod called to say he had work to do on his property and would not be in the store. However, he expected a package from a certain company; and wanted someone to call him if it arrived. Saturdays having become their busiest time, Fridays were slow. Joey and Sara left the store in the early afternoon since they were participating in another revival a few towns from there, north of Charleston. An hour before closing Kailynn signed for the package. She pressed the numbers on the telephone, calling Rod's house, but no one answered. She tried his cell phone, but still no response.

Locking up, she decided to deliver the package to the Webster's house. Skittish at first about driving the Toyota, she felt comfortable as she drove along the residential streets. As she turned into the drive she spotted Milly and Taylor in jersey and jeans playing ball with Stewart on the side lot. As she stepped out of the vehicle, they all three came running over to greet her, the black lab wagging his tail excitedly. She knelt down to look into the dog's brown eyes full of love and kindness; and putting the package down, she wrapped her arms around his big, stocky shoulders. He nuzzled the back of her neck with his nose before pulling back and rubbing his teddy-bear head against her legs, begging her to pet him. He missed her, too.

"Wanna play ball, Kailynn?" Milly asked.

"Sorry, not in this skirt and blouse." Kailynn patted the silky peach material. "I'll take a raincheck. Okay?"

"Sure thing," Taylor said, his eyes saying he took it as a promise.

"Where is your Dad?" She picked up the package as she stood, and waved it.

"Let's find him." Taylor led her into the living room where she immediately noticed the painting of the flower garden over the mantle.

"Your Dad's artwork?" she asked.

"Yes!" Milly answered proudly. "Mommy's portrait is upstairs between Taylor's and my room. I can pick fresh flowers for the vase every day!"

"That's good, Milly." Kailynn looked thoughtful.

"Daddy!" Milly called through the house.

"He must be working out in the garden," Taylor suggested.

"You have a garden this year?" Kailynn felt heartened by the improvement in family life.

Taylor's eyes twinkled as he informed her, "Two. A small vegetable and a large flower garden. Go on out there. Milly and I will make some ice tea." He encouraged her to move through the kitchen with them, letting her out through the door alone. She took in the scintillating sight and scent of award winning roses – red, pink and yellow-glowing in the moisture of the installed sprinklers. A variety of tall flowers and ornamental grass lined stone steps ascending the hill. Delight turned to dismay as a troublesome thought crept into her mind. Has Rod transformed the location into a shrine for his departed wife? Climbing the steps, she saw him garbed in a blue denim shirt and jeans, positioning a redwood picnic table. She noticed comfortable redwood chairs and a glider. A stone bird bath centered a circle of low lying flowers under the maple tree.

Suddenly, aware of her presence, he straightened up.

She was conscious of an honest longing lending a deepening hue to his blue eyes and giving a determined set to his mouth and strong chin. "Your…your package came. I tried…I tried to call." Appalled by her weak attempt to explain her presence there, she blushed. In her ears, the tone sounded like she was making an excuse.

Without taking his eyes off her face he answered, his voice low, but stronger than she had ever heard it. "The cell is charging in the house."

Still looking at him as if he might disappear, she offered the package.

His strong, warm and gentle hand covered her slender fingers as he took hold of the parcel.

"Kailynn," he said her name low and tenderly.

"Yes?"

"Don't leave. It's so good to see you here again."

Only the chirping birds and fluttering breeze answered for her.

Since she hadn't let go of the package, his hand enveloped hers. "You lift our spirits, Kailynn. You give us joy." He paused. "We need you." He lowered his eyelids at this point, and squeezed her hand. "I need you."

She, too, had lowered her gaze to their hands; but now that he was raising his eyelids again, she searched his face. When his gaze shifted to her lips, she let go of the package, and took a step back.

Putting the package on the table, he reached into a pocket of his jeans; and held out a small box in the palm of his hand. "I've been carrying this ring every day, Kailynn. Please don't say no!"

She beheld a lovely solitaire diamond in awe, her mind trying to process his words. All she could think at the moment is that he could have lost it!

He took her left hand to slip the ring on her finger. They both looked at the ring and their hands together. "Please marry me."

She tried to speak, but her throat felt too tight and dry.

Looking frustrated, he now pleaded, "Don't you see? We make each other happy when we're together!"

He astonished her by scrambling down the steps to the rose bed where he took his pocket knife to cut a stem. Taking the steps two at a time, he held out a red rose to her. He observed her surprise, her green eyes glistening with tears as she took the rose. This time he searched her face. His voice was soft and his impediment pronounced. "Do you love me, Kailynn?" He held his breath.

Her heart melted in amazement and loosened her tongue. She smiled and reached a hand up to stroke the side of his face. "Yes, Rod, I love you." Looking earnestly into his eyes she whispered, "With every beat of my heart."

He was silent for a moment as they gazed at each other. His voice sounded stronger when he finally spoke. "I love you, Kailynn! Will you *please* marry me?"

She whispered, "Yes." Throwing her head back, she wrapped her arms around his neck and laughed joyfully. "Yes, Rod! I will marry you!"

He gently pulled her close to him and kissed her lips.

A duet of voices rang out, "Yay!!"

Smiling, Rod and Kailynn turned to see his two children in an upstairs window, giving each other a high-five.

As the couple descended the steps from the hill and moved toward the house, arm in arm, the children ran out to meet them. Milly threw her arms wide to both of them, and Taylor approached them with a big smile spread across his face, but caught himself up short before grabbing them in the bear hug he would have naturally enjoyed.

As they all turned to go through the back door, Kailynn stopped. Looking at Taylor, she informed them, "I refuse to enter this home's doorway again without a genuine welcome hug from my favorite young man."

Using his best John Wayne impression, Taylor responded. "Okay, little lady Miss Kay, I aim to please." He was awarded with her delighted laughter as he slipped an arm about her shoulders, and hugged her to him.

They all busied themselves in the kitchen chopping up onions, warming up chili and preparing side dishes of baked beans and macaroni salad while Rod grilled hot dogs in celebration. He would have liked steak, but there was no time to thaw the packages or marinate before dinner. Having decided to eat at the table on the deck, they bowed their heads when Rod thanked the Lord for their reunion and asked the blessing on the food. Sipping their iced tea, the couple grinned at each other as the youngsters dived into the food.

When Taylor and Milly had gone to their rooms to prepare for bed, the couple sat down on the living room couch with coffee mugs in hand to discuss plans to announce their engagement with their relatives and close friends. Deciding a dinner there at the house would be best, the conversation turned to their personal struggles with the past, sharing their hearts. Since they were being open and forthright, Rod began telling her about the telephone calls conveying Emma's voice, the note with her handwriting and finally the figure gliding into the shadows.

Kailynn knew of the note but now the unidentified calls when no one said anything made sense to her. She sat in fascination, but some alarm as he described the sound of windchimes under his bedroom window and the swishing sound as he followed the figure into the shadows on the hill where it disappeared. "Are the children aware of any of this activity?"

Rod brought himself back from his mental re-enactment with a troubled look. "No, thank the Lord. They don't know anything about these incidents, and I want to keep it that way."

She nodded, and sat quietly in thought for a few minutes.

"That reminds me, I should check on them to make sure they are in bed and asleep."

"Perhaps I should go, then."

"No, Kailynn, not yet. Not after we just talked about these troubling occurrences."

"Okay, I'll stay a little longer. Mind if I call Mother to let her know where I am?"

"By all means, go ahead. I'll only be a few minutes."

Rod saw that Milly's bedroom door was open, and she was already rolled onto her side and asleep with a faint smile on her face. He smiled, too, at the contented expression on her face, as he softly closed the door. He opened Taylor's door just a crack, reluctant to disturb his son's privacy. The boy lay sprawled face down across the covers of his bed, one arm slung over his head, still in his jeans and tee-shirt. Rod grinned and shut the door as quietly as he could manage. Just then, the telephone began ringing. Fearing it would wake the children, he dashed into his room and grabbed the receiver off the charger.

"Hello," he whispered.

"Please come join me…" Emma's voice invited before he slammed the phone down.

His ears picked up the sound of windchimes under his window. He felt like he was losing his mind, but anger soon replaced the confusion. He jerked a small flashlight out of his bedside table and raced down the stairs, meeting Kailynn at the bottom.

"Rod, I'm hearing windchimes."

"I know." He passed her and hurried to the kitchen door, she right behind him.

Once outside, they slowed their pace when the mysterious form of the woman came into view, and silently motioned to each other. Kailynn followed the figure to the steps of the hill while Rod moved around to the other side. The lights from a distant streetlamp and a few windows only created silhouettes and shadows of tree limbs as the three moved stealthily through the night. Though there was no breeze, windchimes tinkled in the night air. As Kailynn neared the top of the hill, the woman disappeared until she saw the beam from Rod's flashlight scanning the other side of the hill. The figure was halfway down the slope.

Rod waited, flashlight in hand, ready to turn it in whatever direction needed if he heard a person descending the hill. Though he imagined his heart was thudding so hard and loud the neighbors should hear it, he was determined to uncover the truth about this supposed supernatural visitor. Suddenly, he heard footsteps scrambling down the slope, and he switched the flashlight on the highest setting. Startled, the woman turned around only to see Kailynn at the top looking down at her. Turning back toward Rod, the light displayed her hazel eyes causing him to gasp. As he drew closer the rest of her features were displayed.

"Nadine?" he whispered.

The woman stood motionless for a few seconds before pulling the wig off her head, and held it and the windchimes in front of her.

"How could you hurt me like this, Nadine?"

She bowed her head, muttering, "I'm sorry, Rod."

"Why would you do this kind of thing to me? We've always been close."

She glared at him then. "Emma didn't want to go that night, Rod. She told me over the phone that she would rather stay home, but you insisted on going and she didn't want you to go alone. She was my baby sister, Rod. While Mom's lower back was out of alignment after her birth, I was the one who took care of her. I watched her grow up. She was like a daughter to me. Your foolishness took her away from her family and me. I couldn't let you forget her, and go merrily about your life."

"I couldn't ever *forget* Emma! The children will never forget her, either. But do you really think that Emma would be pleased with your shenanigans, or glad that we have grieved for so long we forgot how to live and be happy?"

She swallowed the knot in her throat, and her voice cracked. "No...*No*...She would be horrified." A sob shattered the quiet of the night. "Oh Rod! Forgive me! *Please*!" She shook her head. "I've gone too far, haven't I? Things will never be the same between us!"

"Come here, Nadine. I *do* forgive you, Honey," he assured her. "Sometimes, we do crazy things or don't do much of anything when we grieve for a loved one lost to us."

Flinging herself into his arms, she cried on his shoulder as he patted her back.

"Now I want you to come into the house with us, have coffee, and tell me exactly how you managed to do all these things without my realizing it was you."

She wiped her eyes with her hands. "Okay, but you're going to think I was insane and silly. I was acting childish, not like an adult or a loving sister-in-law and aunt. I'm thoroughly ashamed of myself."

"Well, even though it caused me great pain and confusion, I'm curious to know how you pulled all this off."

She shook her head in resignation. "I could use that coffee."

Having made her way down the slope while the two of them had confronted each other, Kailynn joined them as they walked to the house.

Once they were settled around the kitchen table with their coffee mugs full, Rod began questioning his sister-in-law. "Okay, I can see how you dressed to look like Emma at a distance and in the dim lights, but how did you sound exactly like her on the phone? I don't mind telling you that voice was unnerving to me."

Kailynn recognized Emma's yellow dress in the video she had viewed.

Gripping the mug a little tighter, Nadine pressed her lips together before answering his question. "This dress is one Emma left at my house along with a few other articles of clothing the last time she visited. I'm ashamed to admit her voice was meant to shock you and make you nervous."

"But *how-*"

"Emma had left messages on my answering machine, and I simply recorded her invitation on my phone."

"But the caller ID was blank, Nadine. Your name and cell number never appeared."

"I purchased another phone, a disposable phone, and blocked my number from being seen."

Rod sat back in his chair and took a sip of his coffee, considering her actions. "And the note in her handwriting?"

"It was taken from a letter she had written me, tucked inside a greeting card." Nadine smiled sadly as she remembered. "Emma was always placing a PS at the end of her letters, asking me to join her at any event she wanted to attend or actually planned to participate. That one was on a separate sheet of paper."

He nodded. "I still find it hard to believe that you devised all these ways to get my attention, and brought yourself to the point of carrying each one out. Do you hate me?" Seeing the stricken look on her face, he quickly added, "I mean, is it possible that you will continue to harbor ill feelings toward me?"

"No, Rod!!" Her dark eyes were wide with alarm. "Please don't think that! I tell you I was mixed up with missing my baby sister. I didn't want her to be dead and gone from our lives. It was foolish of me, but I didn't want you to forget her and possibly start a life with another woman. I didn't want to lose my brother-in-law." She lowered her head. "I guess I can't expect you to understand such crazy thinking on my part. I'm not sure I understand it, myself."

"In a way I do, Nadine." He scooted forward, stretching his arms on the table while both hands wrapped around his coffee mug. "I felt the same way. I wouldn't allow myself to forget Emma for one second of each day. As time passed, I forced myself to remember the smallest details of our life together and the way she did things. The only thing I couldn't tolerate was the sound of her many windchimes. The sound haunted my dreams and left me with an unbearable emptiness." Examining the thoughtful expression on his sister-in-law's face, he decided to level with her. "I now can see that you had no idea what affect these calls, the note and Emma's appearance had on my mind, but I'm sure a darker spirit was at work when I was tempted with thoughts of joining her in death."

Nadine and Kailynn, both, gasped at his last statement.

Nadine finally found her voice and the courage to say, "But the kids, Rod. Surely you thought about what losing another parent would do to them."

"I wish I could say that I thought of the consequences. But I was too confused and self-absorbed in my grief. What really stopped me was my belief in God, and that I looked forward to eternal life with Him."

Tears welled up in Nadine's eyes. "And I was a tool to push you over the edge of a precipice."

"You didn't know that, Nadine, and you were caught up in your own emotions and grief. You were a victim yourself." Noticing the dubious look on her face, he persisted. "The Bible tells us in Ephesians 6:12 For we wrestle not against flesh and blood, but against principalities, against powers, against the rulers of the darkness of this world, against spiritual wickedness in high places." Relieved to see the reality of this scripture dawn upon her, he assured her, "Come what may, I will always regard you as my sister, and my children will always call you their aunt."

She nodded while the tears overflowed her eyes and streamed down her cheeks.

"Now," Rod continued. "I want the three of us to set our coffee cups down, join hands and pray together for forgiveness, victory and strength to go forward in the joy of the Lord." With that urging, they grasped each other's hands, smiled through their tears, and prayed.

CHAPTER TWENTY-TWO

The excitement generated by the wedding plans produced laughter, sometimes nervous laughter, over the smallest details. Kailynn kept assuring everyone that she was fine with a small, private ceremony and low expenses, but Rod insisted she wear a white wedding dress, saying she deserved to have the best wedding they could possibly pull together. Agnes rushed into the house with a box and secretive whispers as she ushered her to the guest bedroom upstairs. Once inside the room with the door securely closed and locked, she produced a beautiful long white A-line wedding dress.

"Believe it or not, I was once young and slender too," she informed Kailynn with a wink. "I don't think it will need much alteration, but we probably want to pick out a veil, one with delicate white flowers." She stopped her chatter, and looked at Kailynn's surprised expression. "Oh no, have I done it again? Gone ahead and taken charge when I have no business presuming you would want to wear a wedding dress I wore? I'm sorry, darling." Holding the gown up in front of Kailynn, she couldn't resist adding, "I just thought how beautiful you would look, and how proud I would feel when you walked down the aisle in my dress on such a special occasion. I was thinking how honored I would be!" Lifting the dress as if it were a precious baby, she turned toward the box on the bed. "There I go again! I…I…I…I! Will I never change?"

Kailynn placed a hand on Agnes' arm. "Agnes, I'm just overwhelmed with gratitude to imagine you would think that much of me that you would want me to wear your dress. I would be honored beyond words to walk down the aisle in this beautiful gown, knowing how precious it is to you!"

She turned with tears standing in her eyes. "Thank you, Kailynn. God bless you, Honey."

Kailynn hugged her new friend. "He already has."

The day came when Kailynn stood nervously in a little room just inside the door of the sanctuary. She remembered she had shyly wanted a small wedding and was even willing to have it on Rod's property or inside his house, but he insisted they exchange their vows in the church. Smoothing her veil with one hand while she held a small bouquet of pink and white roses in another, she looked down into Milly's smiling face. It helped to calm the little quiver inside her stomach to see the pretty little girl dressed in a pale rose-pink frothy dress, holding her small basket of flowers. No, she wouldn't be alone. She was creating a memory for this precious child, and could straighten her shoulders regally and hold her head high with a genuine smile on her face. When R.L. tapped at the door and opened it for her, she followed Milly through, walking like a princess beside him even though she could see from the corners of her eyes that the entire congregation had gathered to see the couple united in matrimony.

All eyes were turned toward her, and as she began to practically glide down the aisle as if in a dream, keeping time to the wedding march Sara played on the piano, she saw some of the floral arrangements at the end of the pews tied with beautiful pale-pink ribbons. Faltering for a moment, her vision cleared as she looked straight ahead toward Rod, standing tall and handsome in his dark suit, gazing at her as if she were the only person in the room and smiling in admiration. As she neared him, she caught a glimpse of her mother sitting on the front pew beside Nadine and Agnes, and her heart burst with pride as she envisioned her father walking beside her, pleased that she was well and happy.

Taking her place beside the groom, she was encouraged to see Joey standing up as best man. Taylor as the ring-bearer looked older than his years in his new navy-blue suit. Carla stood near her in a rose-pink suit, smiling support Kailynn's way. Hearing a soft cough from the pastor, all five looked toward him as he stood in front of the pulpit.

The pastor stretched out his arms as if presenting the couple, and said in the warmest tones of voice, "We are gathered here today to unite this couple in the sacred bond of marriage."

Suddenly, a current of happiness coursed through Kailynn to the extent that she felt her heart beating harder and heat rushing up to her ears causing a sensation like nerve deafness. Most of the pastor's words were drowned out by the gigantic, undulating waves of inner sounds. The only time these sounds subsided was when the couple faced each other, and Rod held her left hand after she had given her bouquet to Carla to hold. As she looked into his eyes, the only sounds she heard were his vows.

His eyes were pools of dark blue where she submerged her consciousness as he declared with earnest commitment, "I, Roderick Webster, take you, Kailynn

Richardson, as my wife, to have and to hold, for better or worse, in sickness and in health from this day forward."

Taylor produced the ring like a man on a mission, and Rod slipped the gold wedding band on her third finger.

She noticed that he did not speak of death. In turn, she spoke her vows so exclusively to him that the men and women sitting in the sanctuary leaned toward them in an attempt to hear her recite them. With green flecks sparkling in the irises of her eyes, she looked intently into his penetrating gaze, "I, Kailynn Richardson, take you, Roderick Webster, as my husband, to have and to hold, for better or worse, in sickness and in health from this day forward."

Her own fingers trembled with the excitement she felt as she held his left hand and pushed the ring onto his third finger.

"I now pronounce you husband and wife."

Rod lowered his head and his lips touched hers tenderly.

Almost immediately, joyous piano notes filled the air and the people stood smiling as the couple hurried down the aisle.

Once outside, they stopped before getting into Rod's decorated car for Kailynn to throw the bouquet over her shoulder into the crowd which had followed them. Sara jumped up to catch it and Joey looked down at her with a grin and a wink.

CHAPTER TWENTY-THREE

A beautiful autumn sun shines through prismatic leaves. It is a perfect day for the picnic. Everyone relaxes in slacks and loose shirts, everyone except Mrs. Richardson and her middle sister Ruth Graley, also widowed, who now lives with her. They prefer eating from the plates Kailynn has prepared for them and chatting in the rocking chairs on the new side porch while watching the activity upon the hill.

Everyone appears to enjoy their time together. R.L. sits in one of the redwood chairs, strumming a guitar and singing love songs to Agnes. She is all smiles while setting her apple pies next to the fried chicken and potato salad on the table.

Taylor plays a soft theme on the harmonica whenever the singer takes a break to remember the next lyrics. Milly dances under the maple tree. Long blades of ornamental grass wave in her hands tempting Lady to gracefully caper with her. On the glider, Joey leans over to whisper something in Sara's ear before they look into each other's eyes and laugh at their private joke. Mike is recording everything through his cell phone as Carla tries to discourage little Michael's antics in picking fall flowers. Kailynn pours ice tea for everyone; and then walks over to Rod who, along with Stewart, stands surveying the result of his summer efforts to tear out vines and brush. Arms wrapped around each other, husband and wife observe the view of the valley below and the winding river flowing forward in the distance.

ABOUT THE AUTHOR

Photo Credit: Tommy Ong

West Virginia Poet and Storyteller, Shirley Hedrick Williams was born in Charleston, West Virginia; and spent her childhood in the Dunbar-Charleston-Cross Lanes area. She began writing short stories at the age of 11; started expressing herself in poetic forms using nature themes as analogy at the age of 15. Shirley has published poems in Journals across America through the years and received the title of A West Virginia Ambassador of Poetry for All Peoples as a Member of the West Virginia Poetry Society from the Secretary of State, A. James Manchin in April 1984.

Having worked in a library for 12 years, she knows what readers enjoy from a good story. Recently, she has moved her focus to write Christian Romantic Suspense with her debut novel, Releasing Shadows. She is also the author of *Awakening Crow Moon: and Other Poems and Short Stories.*

Shirley is married and the mother of two grown children – a daughter and a son – both writers. She enjoys trips to scenic mountains, woodlands, and rivers with her family, but her heart will always lie in the hills of West Virginia.

Connect with Shirley at:

ShirleyHedrickWilliams@fireandgracepublishing.com

www.ingramcontent.com/pod-product-compliance
Lightning Source LLC
Chambersburg PA
CBHW052027240626
47153CB00006B/1984